A CARTOON NETWORK ORIGINAL

the POWERPUFF GIRLS

The Time Tie

the A CARTOON NETWORK ORIGINAL
POWERPUFF GIRLS
The Time Tie

Special thanks to Marisa Marionakis and Janet No of Cartoon Network.

For international rights, contact licensing@idwpublishing.com

ISBN: 978-1-68405-100-7

20 19 18 17   1 2 3 4

Ted Adams, CEO & Publisher • Greg Goldstein, President & COO • Robbie Robbins, EVP/Sr. Graphic Artist • Chris Ryall, Chief Creative Officer • David Hedgecock, Editor-in-Chief • Laurie Windrow, Senior Vice President of Sales & Marketing • Matthew Ruzicka, CPA, Chief Financial Officer • Lorelei Bunjes, VP of Digital Services • Jerry Bennington, VP of New Product Development

Facebook: facebook.com/idwpublishing • Twitter: @idwpublishing • YouTube: youtube.com/idwpublishing
Tumblr: tumblr.idwpublishing.com • Instagram: instagram.com/idwpublishing

www.IDWPUBLISHING.com

Originally published as THE POWERPUFF GIRLS: THE TIME TIE issues #1–3.

Art by
Philip Murphy

Written by
Haley Mancini &
Jake Goldman

Colors by
Philip Murphy & **Leonardo Ito**

Letters by
Andworld Productions

Series Edits by
Sarah Gaydos

Series Assistant Edits by
Chase Marotz

Cover by
Chad Thomas

Collection Edits by
Justin Eisinger & **Alonzo Simon**

Collection Design by
Claudia Chong

Publisher: **Ted Adams**

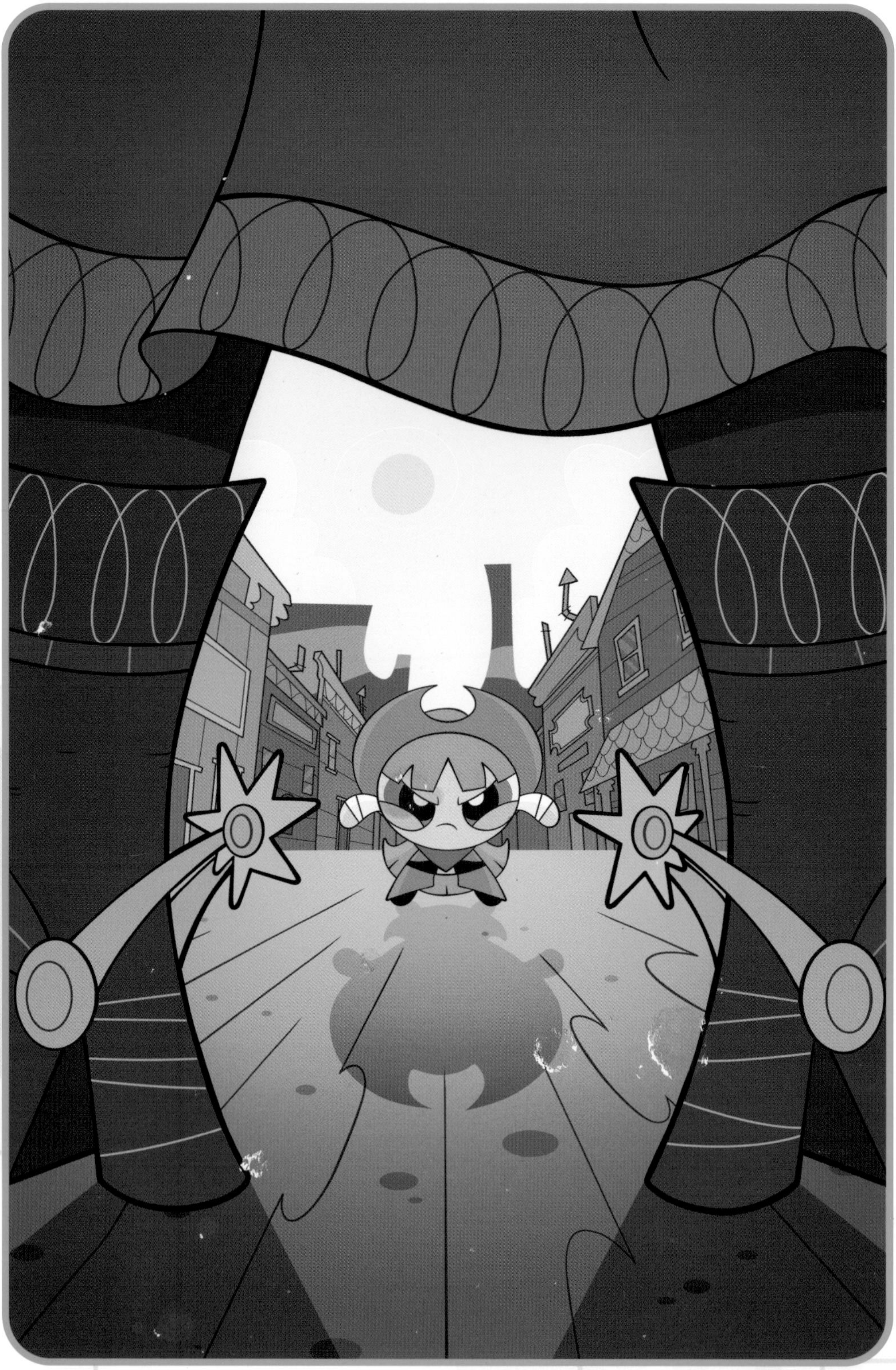

Cover Art by **Philip Murphy**

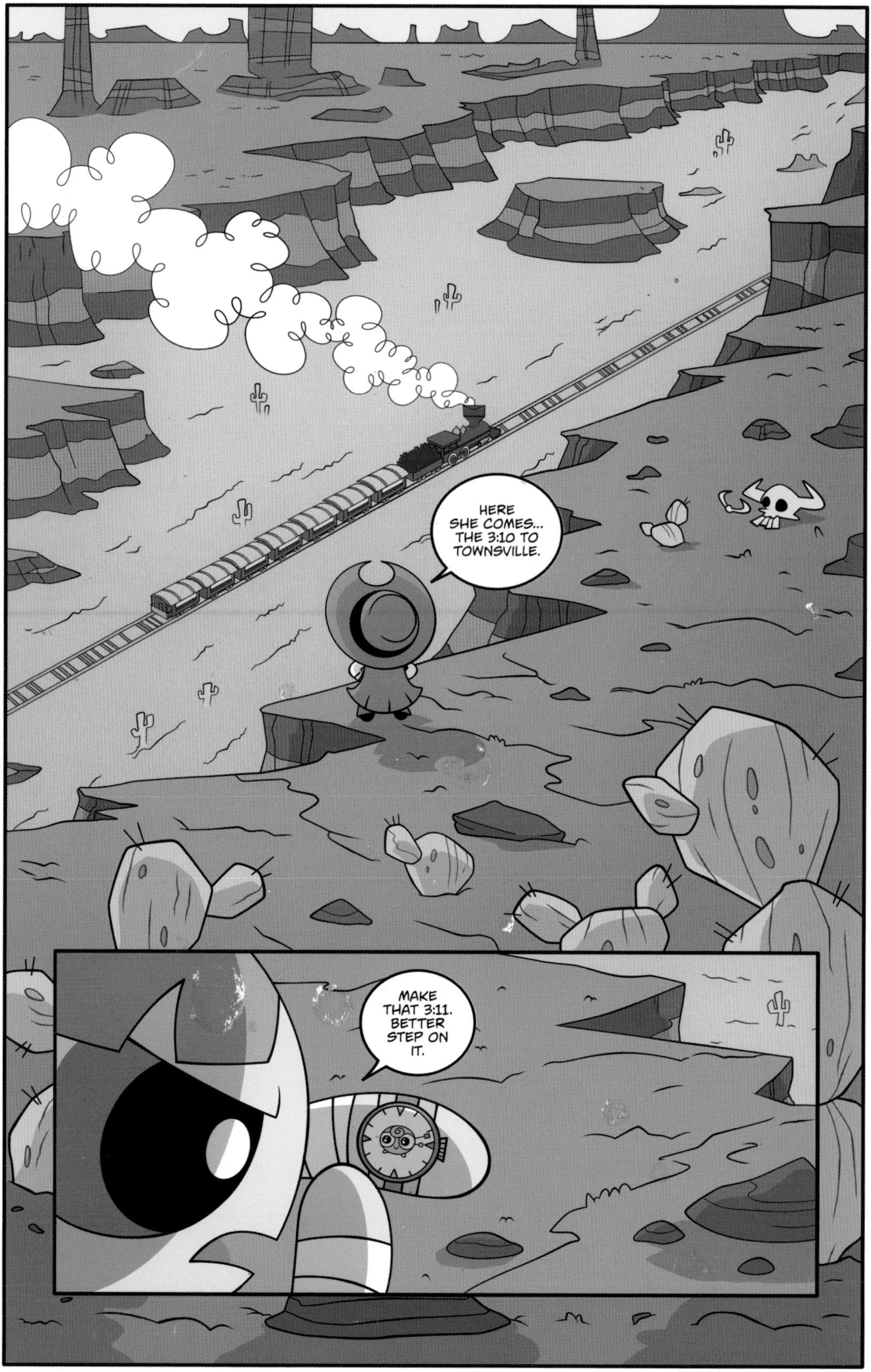
HERE SHE COMES... THE 3:10 TO TOWNSVILLE.
MAKE THAT 3:11. BETTER STEP ON IT.

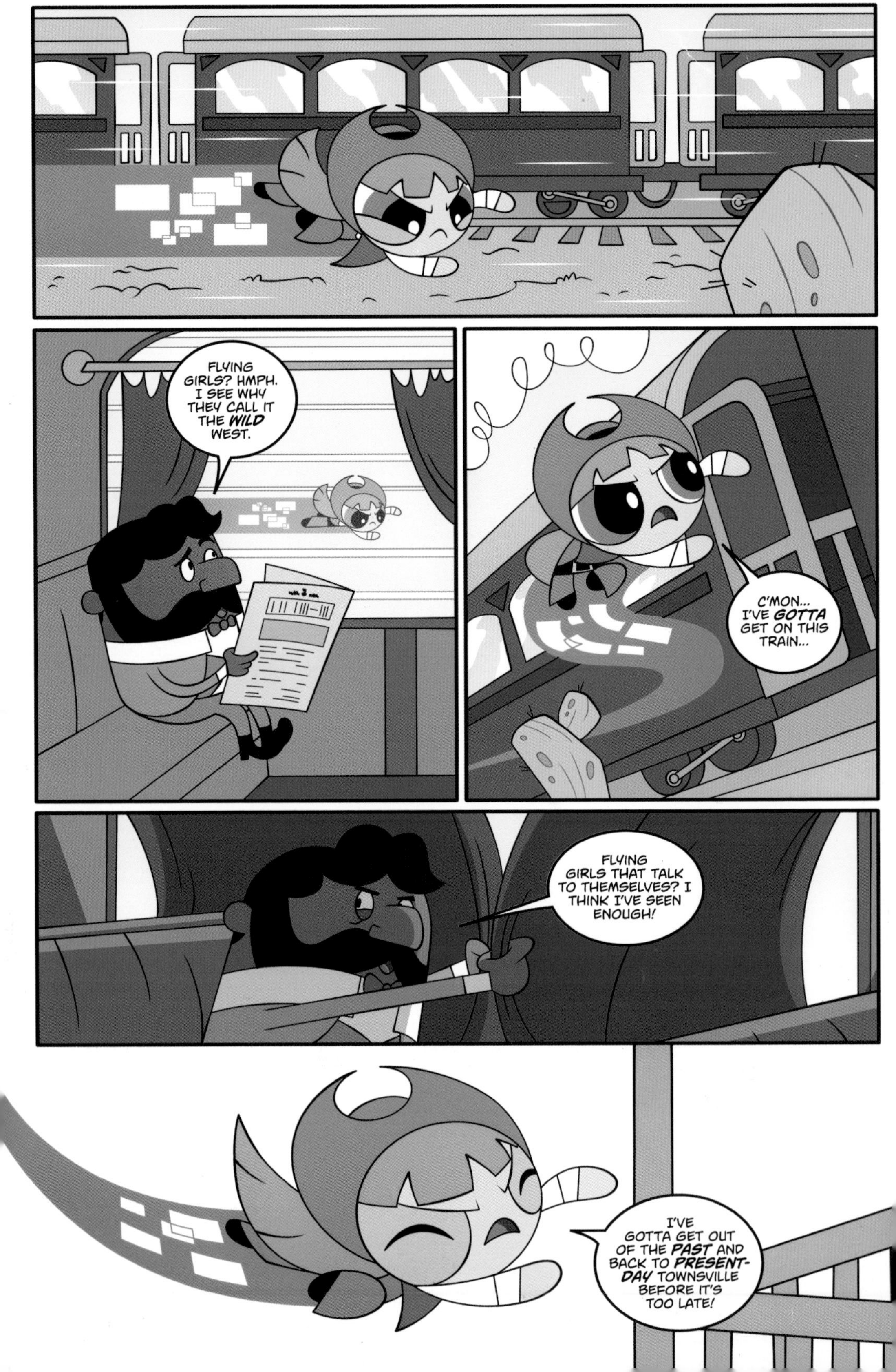
FLYING GIRLS? HMPH. I SEE WHY THEY CALL IT THE *WILD* WEST.
C'MON... I'VE *GOTTA* GET ON THIS TRAIN...
FLYING GIRLS THAT TALK TO THEMSELVES? I THINK I'VE SEEN ENOUGH!
I'VE GOTTA GET OUT OF THE *PAST* AND BACK TO *PRESENT-DAY* TOWNSVILLE BEFORE IT'S TOO LATE!

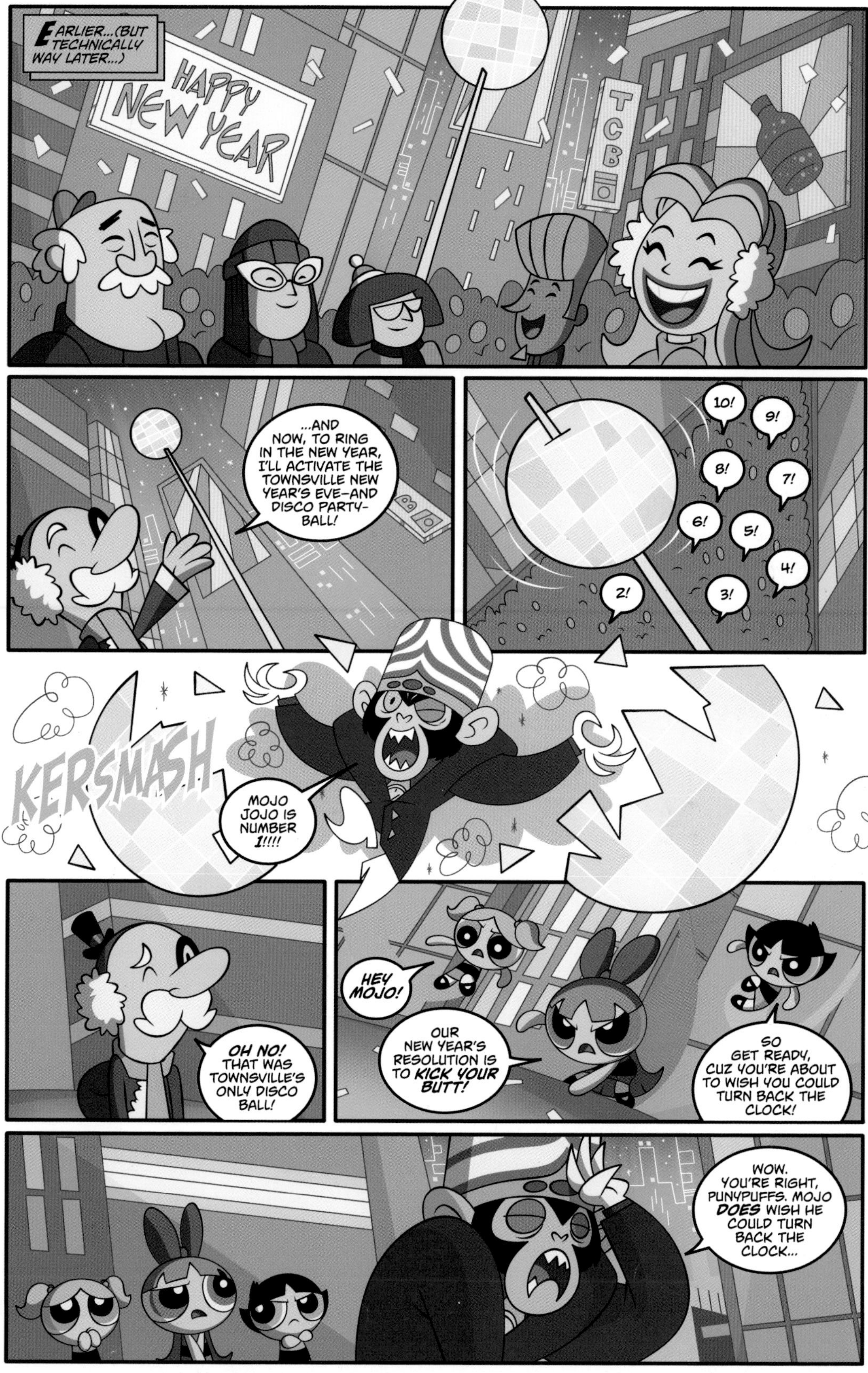
EARLIER...(BUT TECHNICALLY WAY LATER...)
HAPPY NEW YEAR
TCB
...AND NOW, TO RING IN THE NEW YEAR, I'LL ACTIVATE THE TOWNSVILLE NEW YEAR'S EVE–AND DISCO PARTY-BALL!
10!
9!
8!
7!
6!
5!
4!
3!
2!
KERSMASH
MOJO JOJO IS NUMBER 1!!!!
OH NO! THAT WAS TOWNSVILLE'S ONLY DISCO BALL!
HEY MOJO!
OUR NEW YEAR'S RESOLUTION IS TO KICK YOUR BUTT!
SO GET READY, CUZ YOU'RE ABOUT TO WISH YOU COULD TURN BACK THE CLOCK!
WOW. YOU'RE RIGHT, PUNYPUFFS. MOJO DOES WISH HE COULD TURN BACK THE CLOCK...

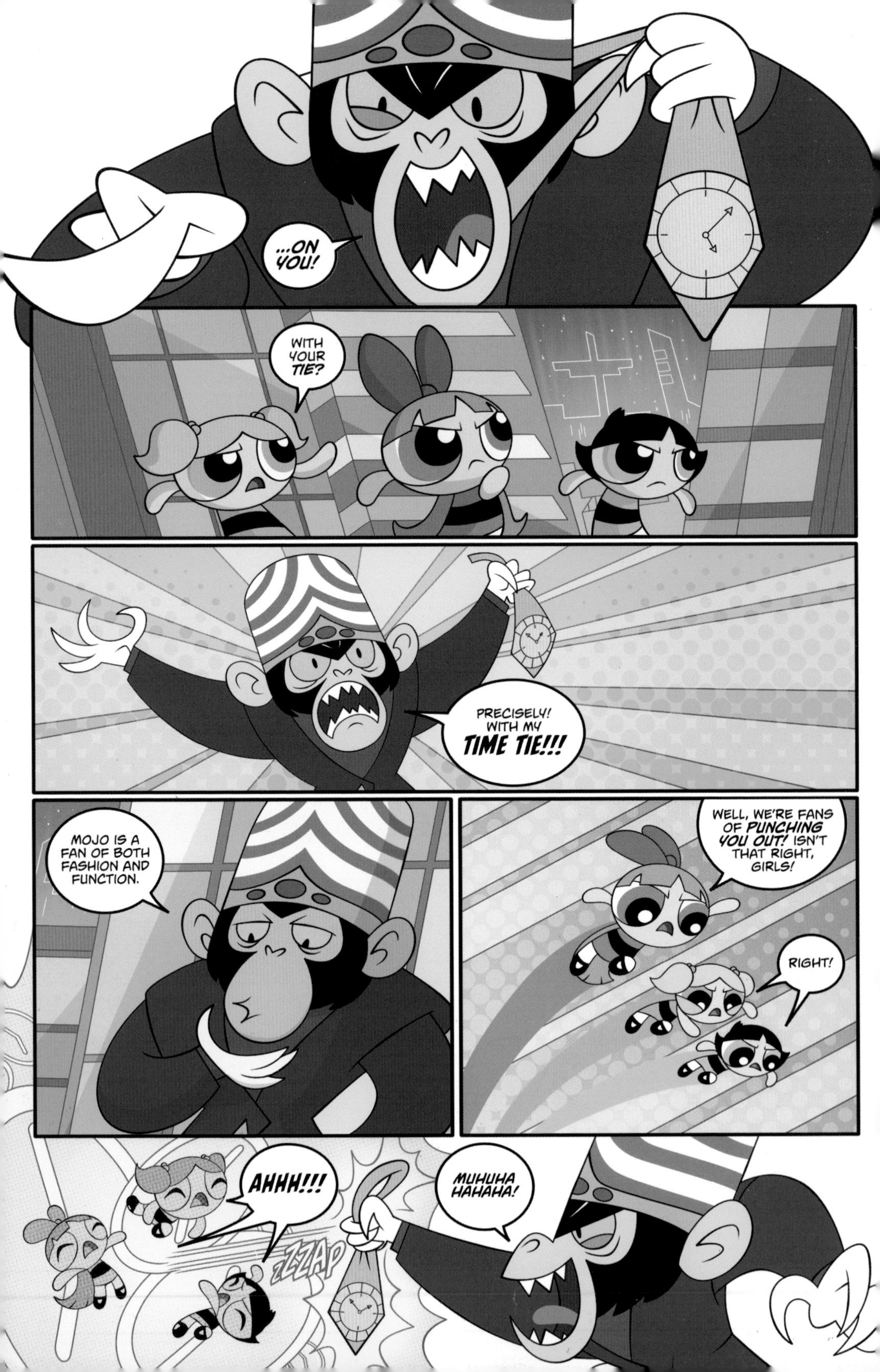
...ON YOU!
WITH YOUR TIE?
PRECISELY! WITH MY TIME TIE!!!
MOJO IS A FAN OF BOTH FASHION AND FUNCTION.
WELL, WE'RE FANS OF PUNCHING YOU OUT! ISN'T THAT RIGHT, GIRLS!
RIGHT!
AHHH!!!
MUHUHA HAHAHA!
ZZZAP

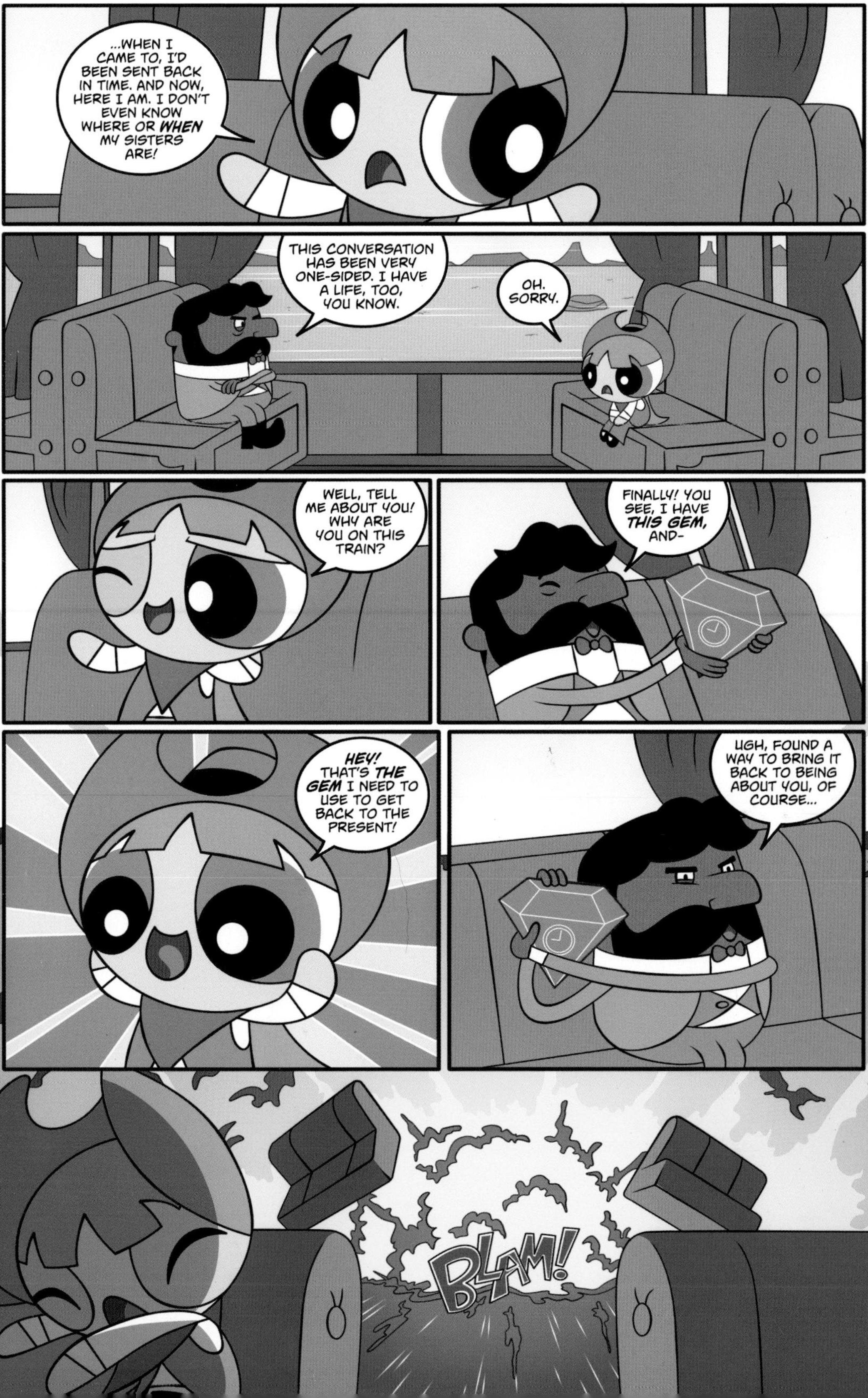
...WHEN I CAME TO, I'D BEEN SENT BACK IN TIME. AND NOW, HERE I AM. I DON'T EVEN KNOW WHERE OR WHEN MY SISTERS ARE!
THIS CONVERSATION HAS BEEN VERY ONE-SIDED. I HAVE A LIFE, TOO, YOU KNOW.
OH. SORRY.
WELL, TELL ME ABOUT YOU! WHY ARE YOU ON THIS TRAIN?
FINALLY! YOU SEE, I HAVE THIS GEM, AND-
HEY! THAT'S THE GEM I NEED TO USE TO GET BACK TO THE PRESENT!
UGH, FOUND A WAY TO BRING IT BACK TO BEING ABOUT YOU, OF COURSE...
BLAM!

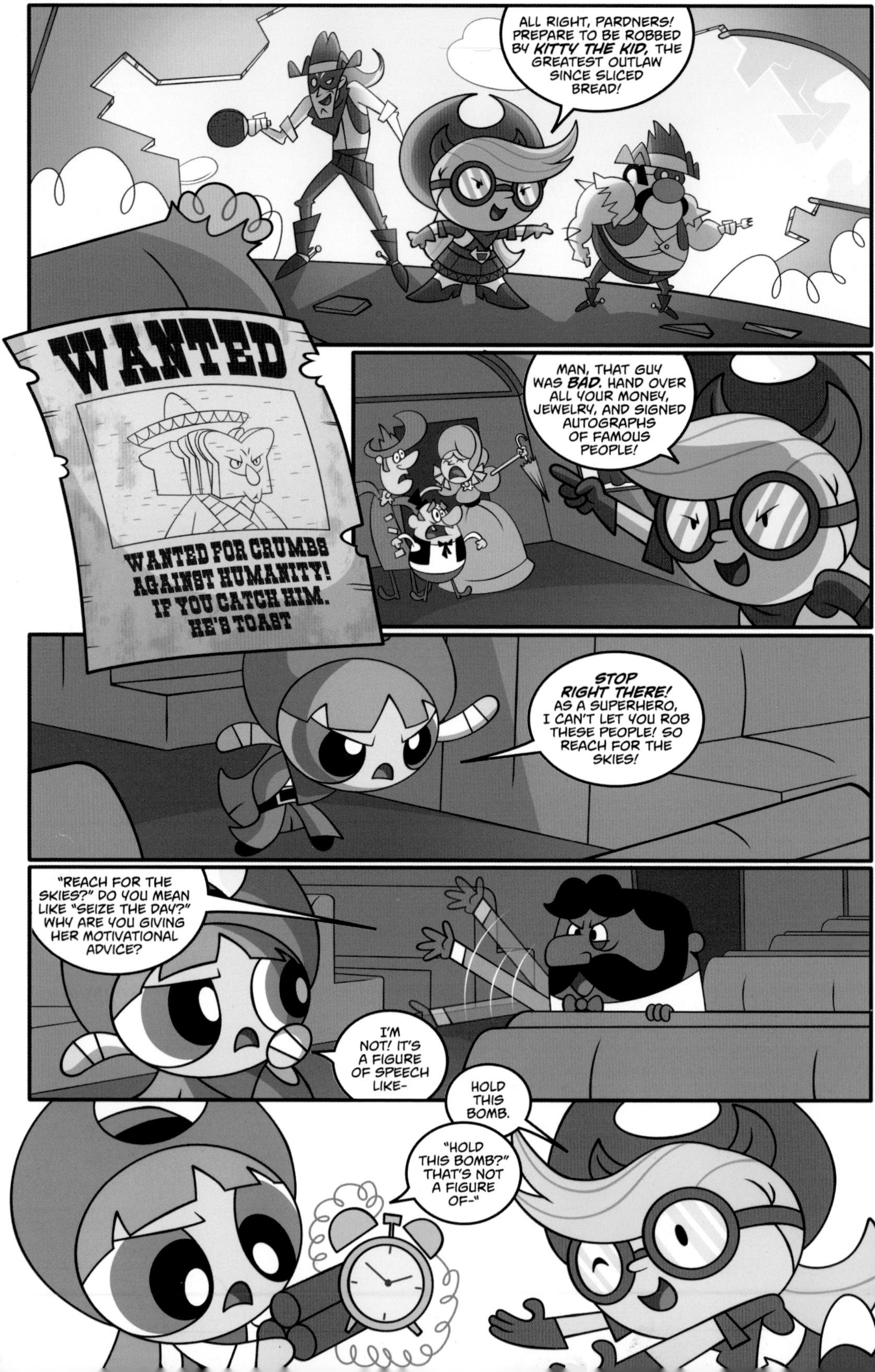
ALL RIGHT, PARDNERS! PREPARE TO BE ROBBED BY KITTY THE KID, THE GREATEST OUTLAW SINCE SLICED BREAD!
WANTED
WANTED FOR CRUMBS AGAINST HUMANITY! IF YOU CATCH HIM. HE'S TOAST
MAN, THAT GUY WAS BAD. HAND OVER ALL YOUR MONEY, JEWELRY, AND SIGNED AUTOGRAPHS OF FAMOUS PEOPLE!
STOP RIGHT THERE! AS A SUPERHERO, I CAN'T LET YOU ROB THESE PEOPLE! SO REACH FOR THE SKIES!
"REACH FOR THE SKIES?" DO YOU MEAN LIKE "SEIZE THE DAY?" WHY ARE YOU GIVING HER MOTIVATIONAL ADVICE?
I'M NOT! IT'S A FIGURE OF SPEECH LIKE-
HOLD THIS BOMB.
"HOLD THIS BOMB?" THAT'S NOT A FIGURE OF-"

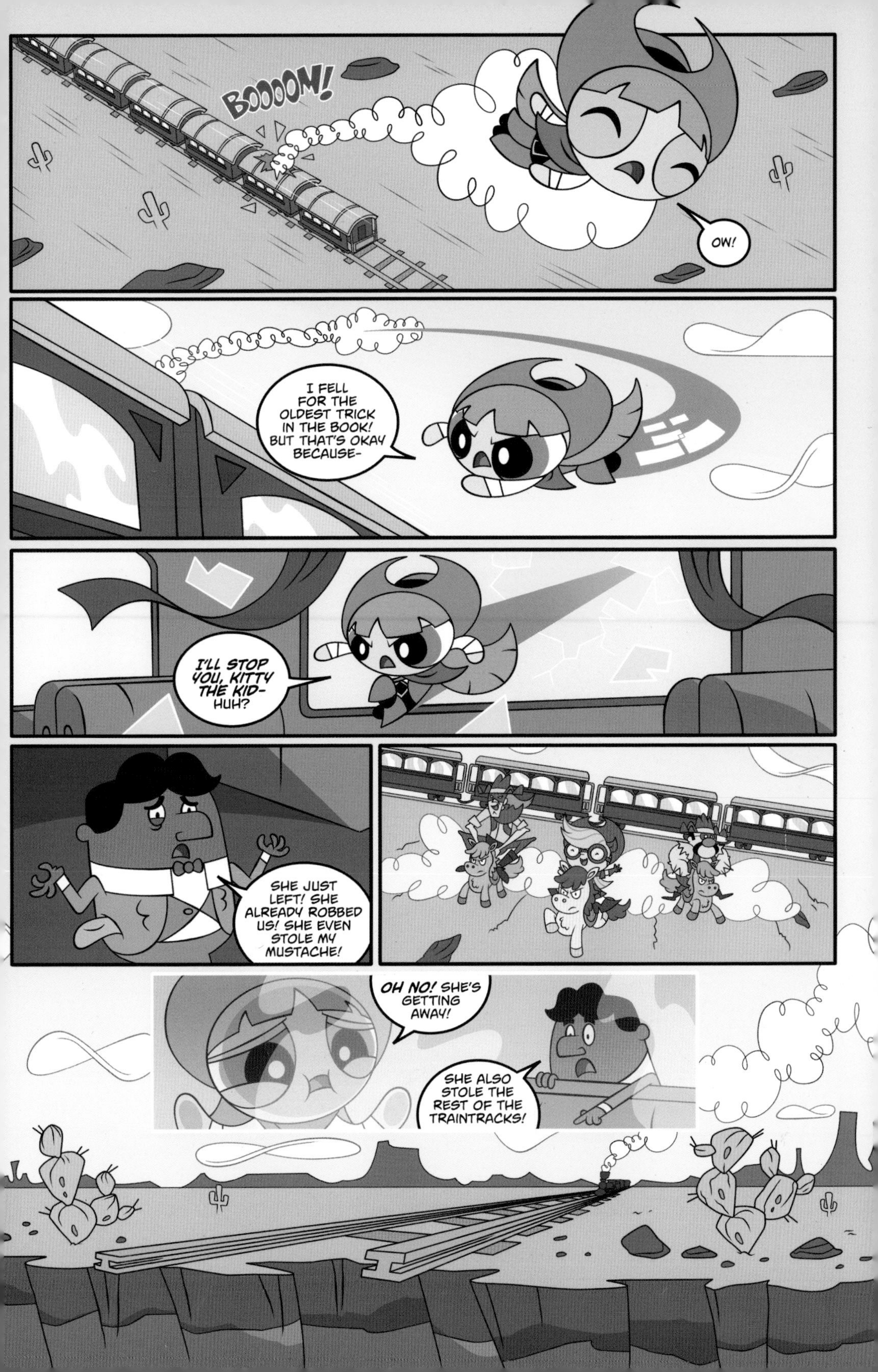
BOOOOM!
OW!
I FELL FOR THE OLDEST TRICK IN THE BOOK! BUT THAT'S OKAY BECAUSE-
I'LL STOP YOU, KITTY THE KID-
HUH?
SHE JUST LEFT! SHE ALREADY ROBBED US! SHE EVEN STOLE MY MUSTACHE!
OH NO! SHE'S GETTING AWAY!
SHE ALSO STOLE THE REST OF THE TRAINTRACKS!

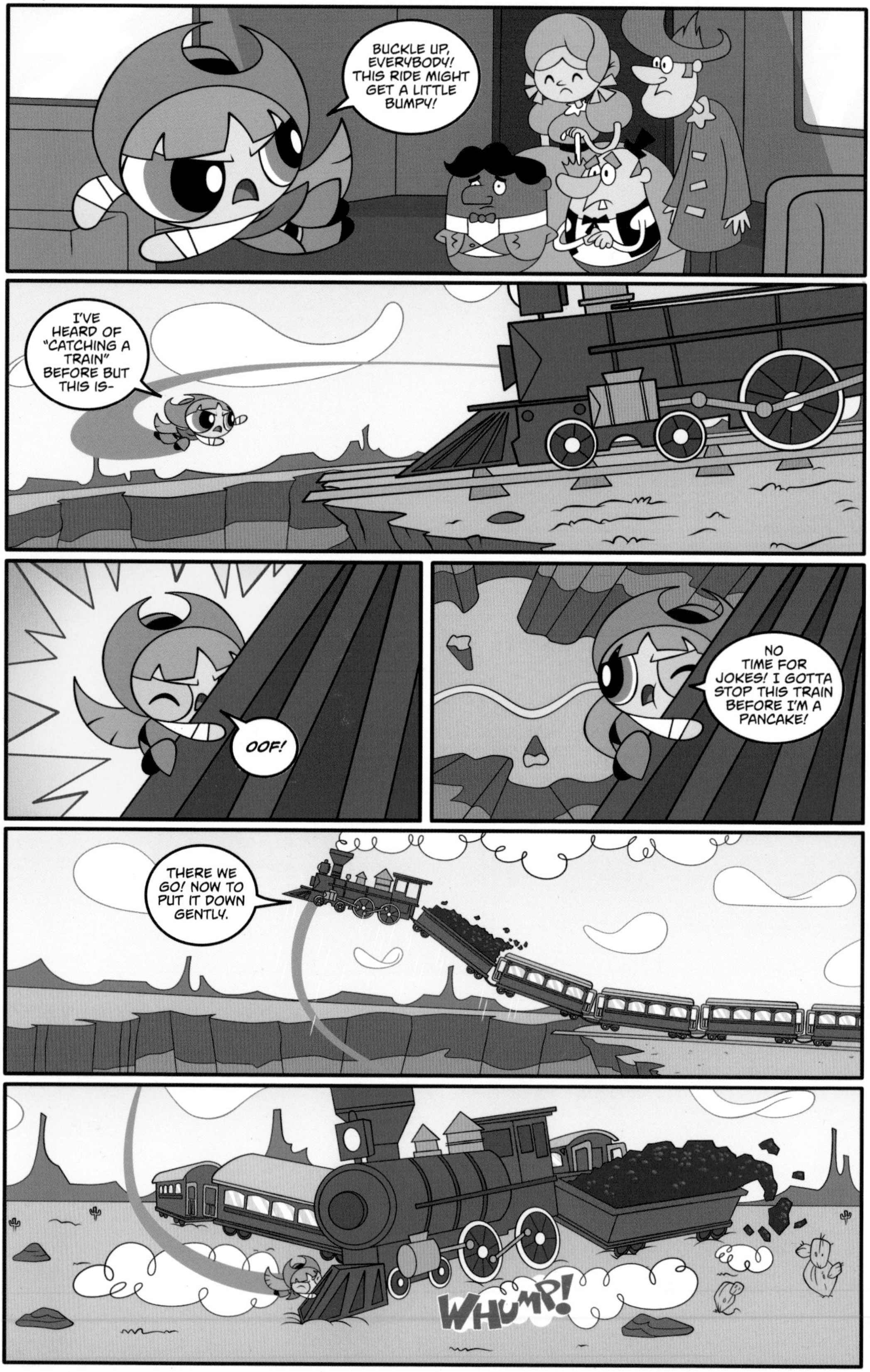
BUCKLE UP, EVERYBODY! THIS RIDE MIGHT GET A LITTLE BUMPY!
I'VE HEARD OF "CATCHING A TRAIN" BEFORE BUT THIS IS-
OOF!
NO TIME FOR JOKES! I GOTTA STOP THIS TRAIN BEFORE I'M A PANCAKE!
THERE WE GO! NOW TO PUT IT DOWN GENTLY.
WHUMP!

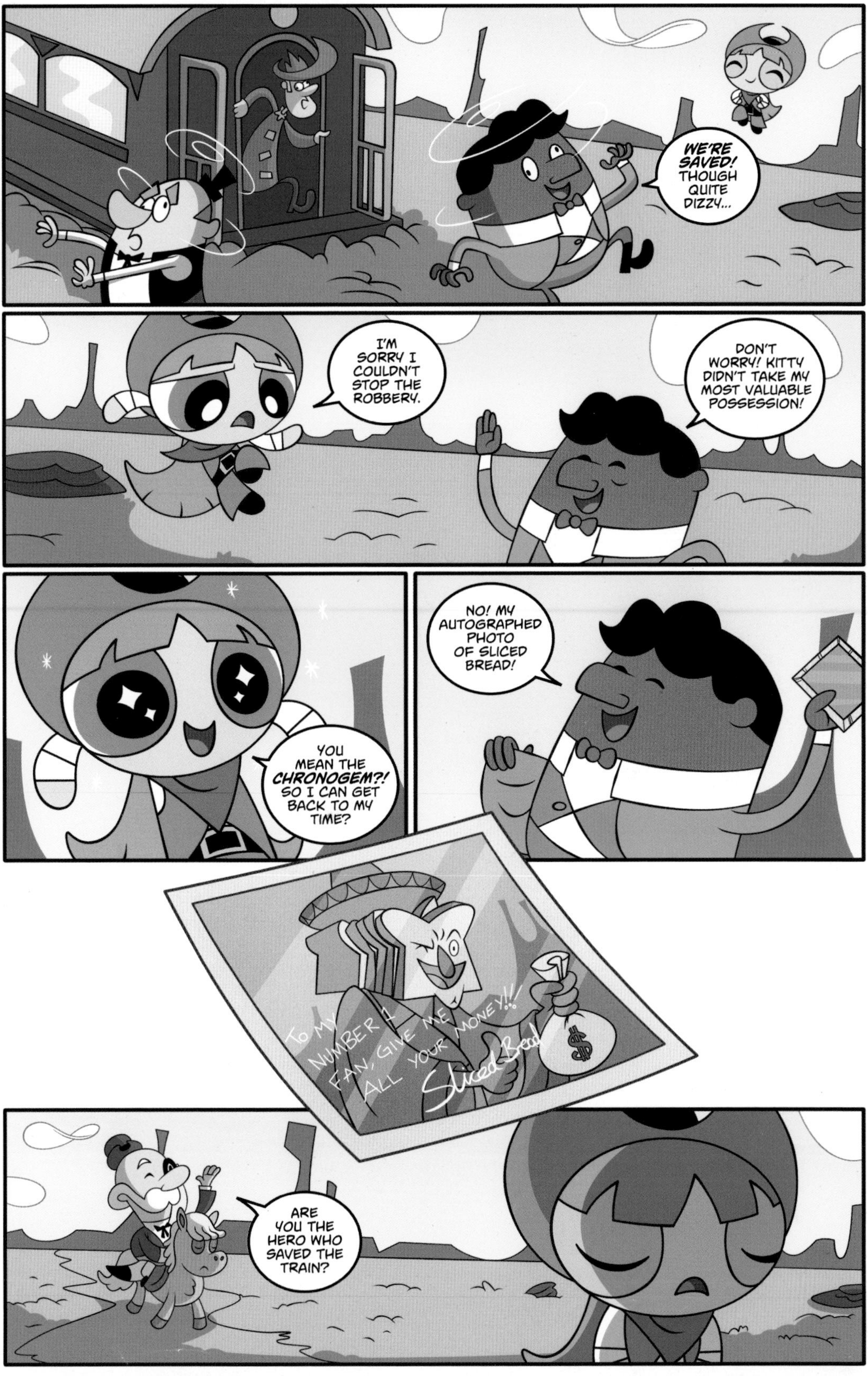
WE'RE SAVED! THOUGH QUITE DIZZY...
I'M SORRY I COULDN'T STOP THE ROBBERY.
DON'T WORRY! KITTY DIDN'T TAKE MY MOST VALUABLE POSSESSION!
YOU MEAN THE CHRONOGEM?! SO I CAN GET BACK TO MY TIME?
NO! MY AUTOGRAPHED PHOTO OF SLICED BREAD!
TO MY NUMBER 1 FAN, GIVE ME ALL YOUR MONEY!!!
Sliced Bread
ARE YOU THE HERO WHO SAVED THE TRAIN?

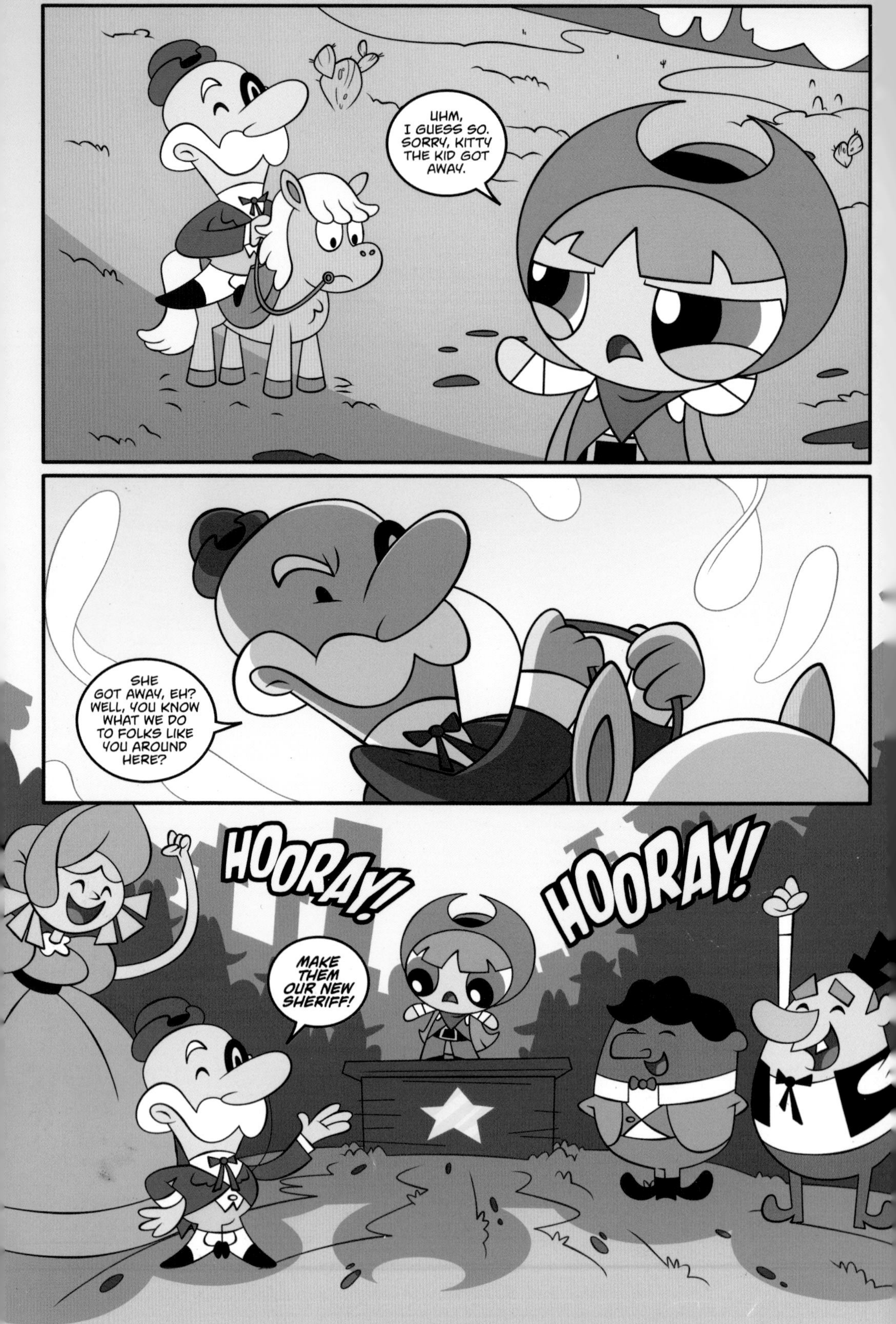
UHM, I GUESS SO. SORRY, KITTY THE KID GOT AWAY.
SHE GOT AWAY, EH? WELL, YOU KNOW WHAT WE DO TO FOLKS LIKE YOU AROUND HERE?
HOORAY!
HOORAY!
MAKE THEM OUR NEW SHERIFF!

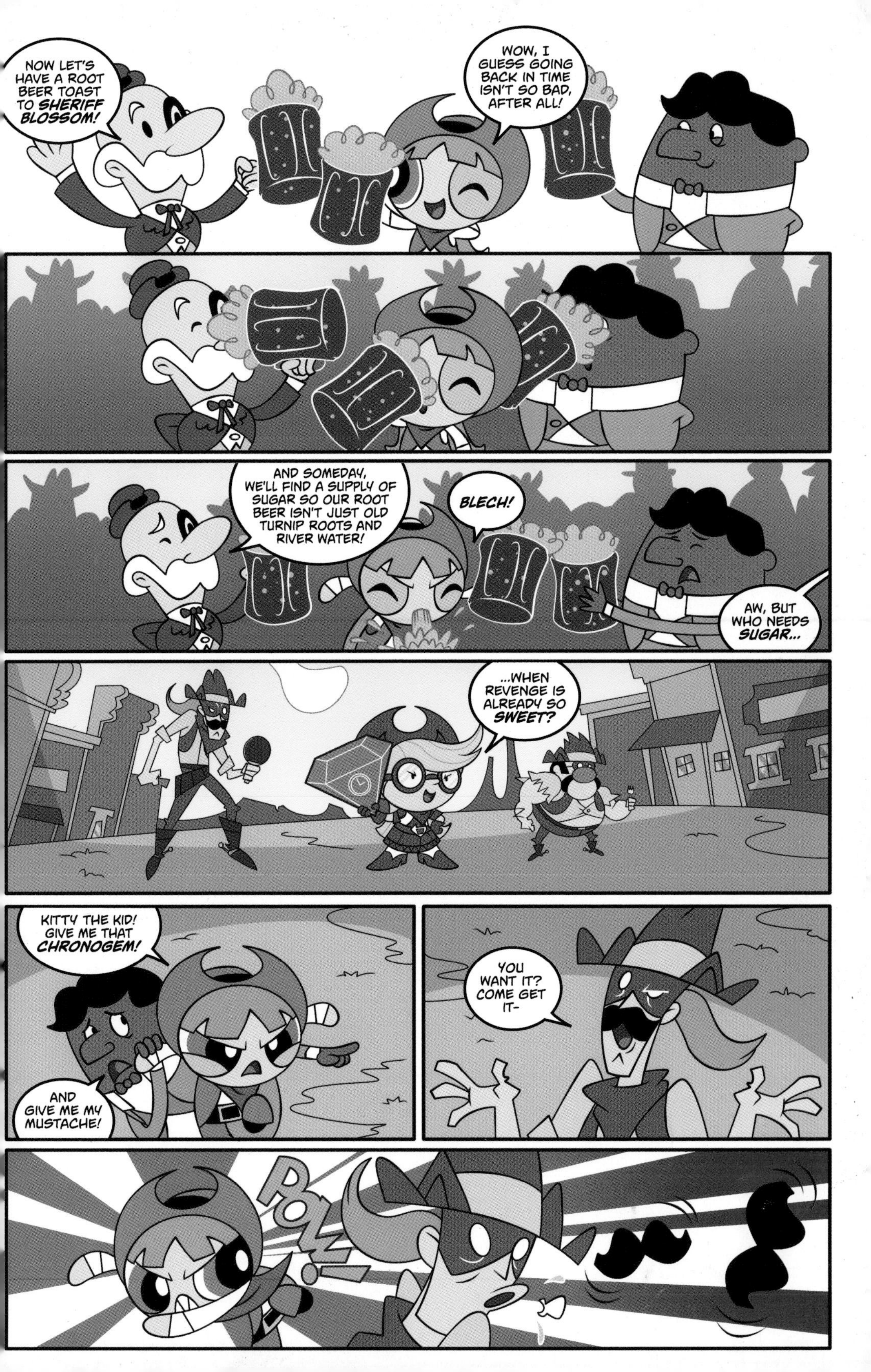
NOW LET'S HAVE A ROOT BEER TOAST TO SHERIFF BLOSSOM!
WOW, I GUESS GOING BACK IN TIME ISN'T SO BAD, AFTER ALL!
AND SOMEDAY, WE'LL FIND A SUPPLY OF SUGAR SO OUR ROOT BEER ISN'T JUST OLD TURNIP ROOTS AND RIVER WATER!
BLECH!
AW, BUT WHO NEEDS SUGAR...
...WHEN REVENGE IS ALREADY SO SWEET?
KITTY THE KID! GIVE ME THAT CHRONOGEM!
AND GIVE ME MY MUSTACHE!
YOU WANT IT? COME GET IT-
POW-

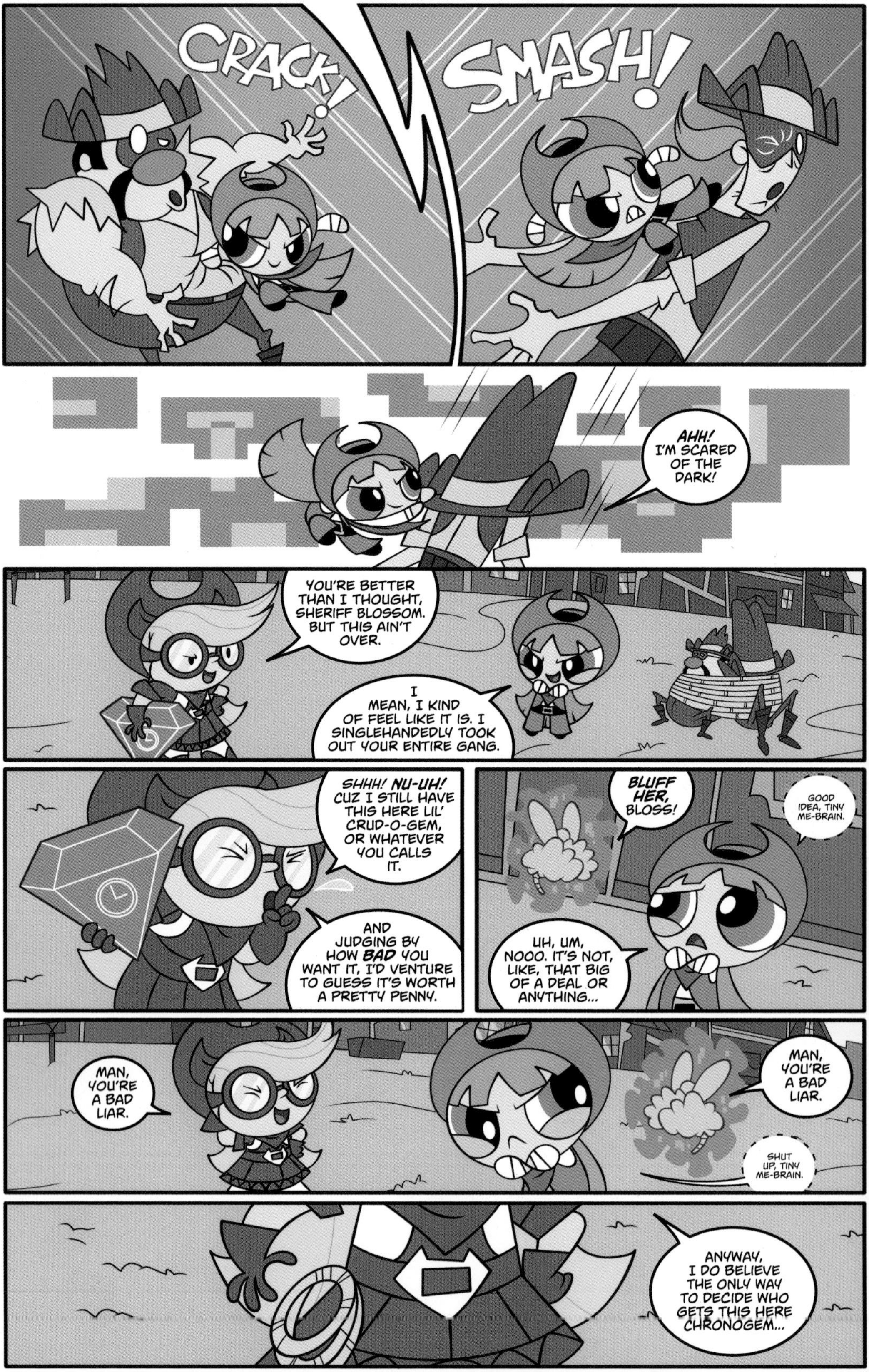

CRACK!
SMASH!
AHH! I'M SCARED OF THE DARK!
YOU'RE BETTER THAN I THOUGHT, SHERIFF BLOSSOM. BUT THIS AIN'T OVER.
I MEAN, I KIND OF FEEL LIKE IT IS. I SINGLEHANDEDLY TOOK OUT YOUR ENTIRE GANG.
SHHH! NU-UH! CUZ I STILL HAVE THIS HERE LIL' CRUD-O-GEM, OR WHATEVER YOU CALLS IT.
AND JUDGING BY HOW BAD YOU WANT IT, I'D VENTURE TO GUESS IT'S WORTH A PRETTY PENNY.
BLUFF HER, BLOSS!
GOOD IDEA, TINY ME-BRAIN.
UH, UM, NOOO. IT'S NOT, LIKE, THAT BIG OF A DEAL OR ANYTHING...
MAN, YOU'RE A BAD LIAR.
MAN, YOU'RE A BAD LIAR.
SHUT UP, TINY ME-BRAIN.
ANYWAY, I DO BELIEVE THE ONLY WAY TO DECIDE WHO GETS THIS HERE CHRONOGEM...

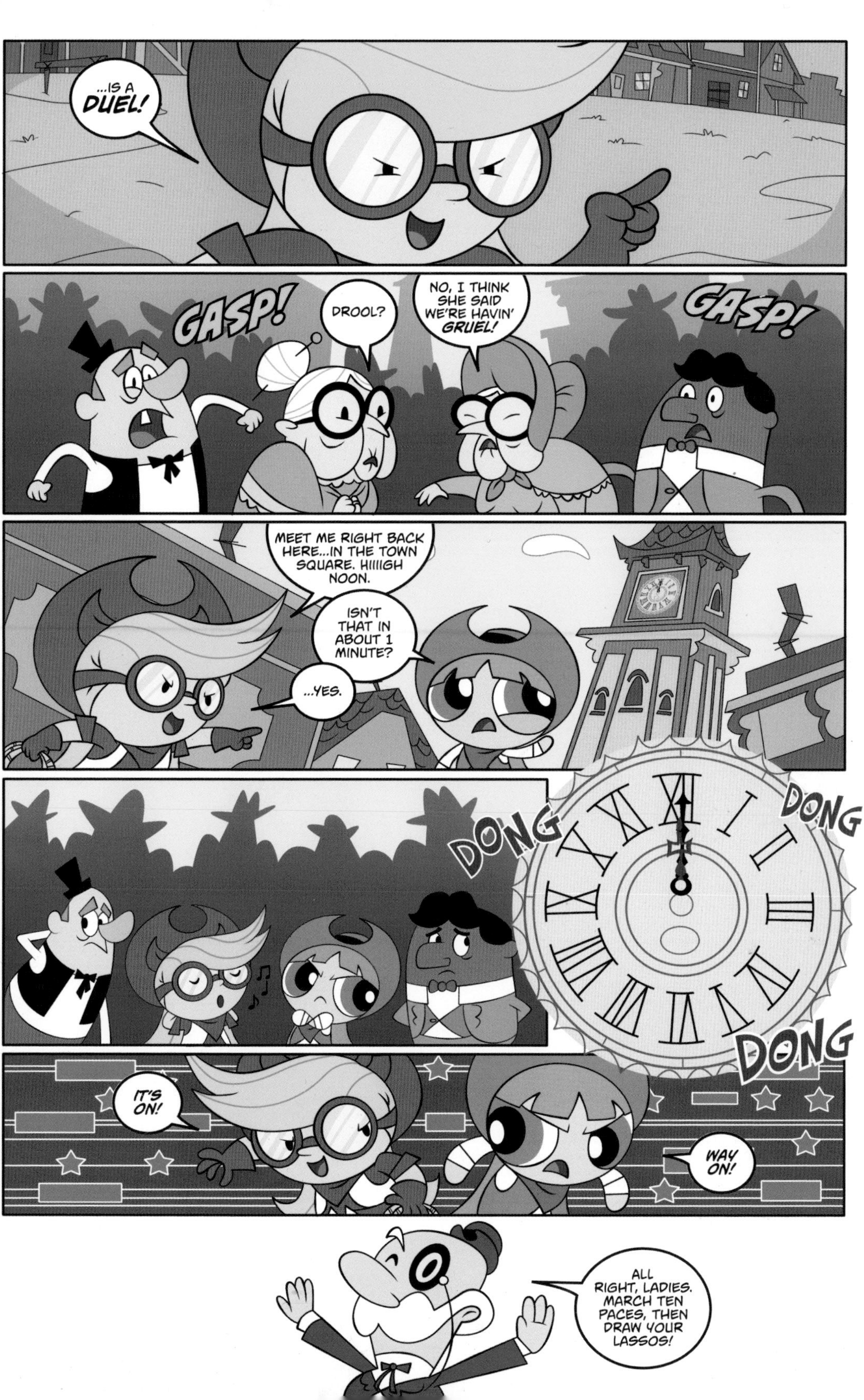
...IS A DUEL!
GASP!
DROOL?
NO, I THINK SHE SAID WE'RE HAVIN' GRUEL!
GASP!
MEET ME RIGHT BACK HERE...IN THE TOWN SQUARE. HIIIIGH NOON.
ISN'T THAT IN ABOUT 1 MINUTE?
...YES.
DONG
DONG
DONG
IT'S ON!
WAY ON!
ALL RIGHT, LADIES. MARCH TEN PACES, THEN DRAW YOUR LASSOS!

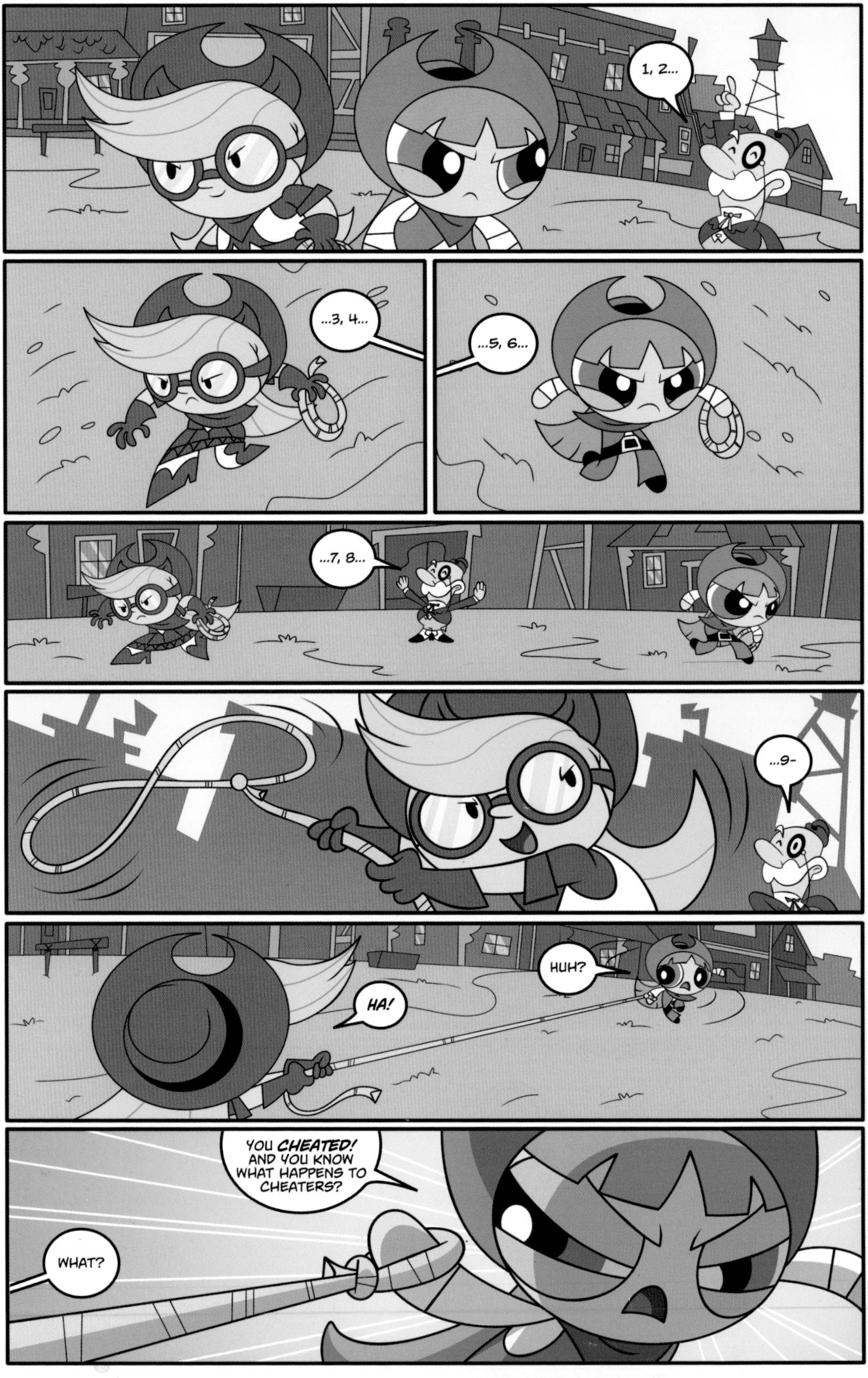
1, 2...
...3, 4...
...5, 6...
...7, 8...
...9-
HUH?
HA!
YOU CHEATED! AND YOU KNOW WHAT HAPPENS TO CHEATERS?
WHAT?

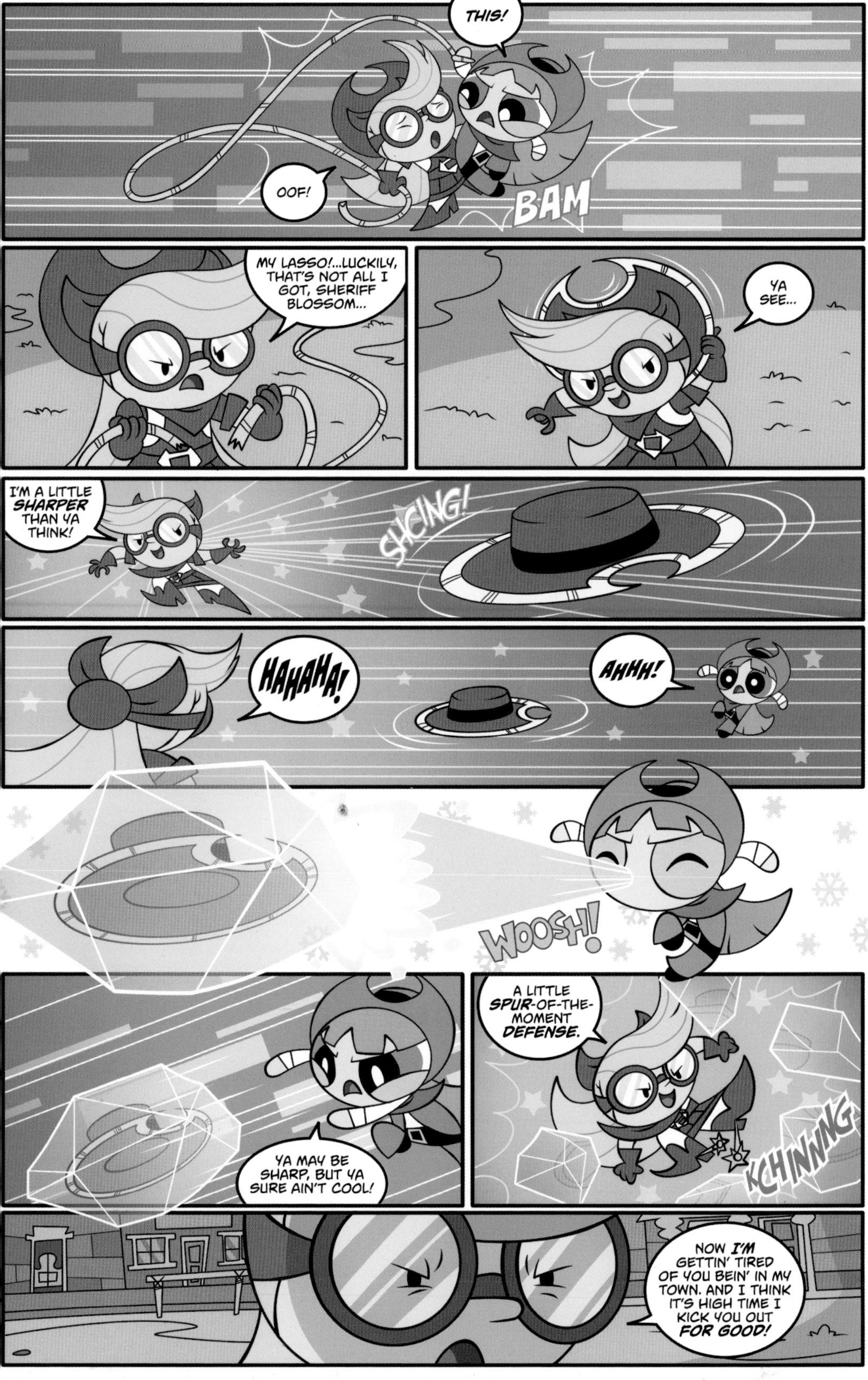
THIS!
OOF!
BAM
MY LASSO!...LUCKILY, THAT'S NOT ALL I GOT, SHERIFF BLOSSOM...
YA SEE...
I'M A LITTLE SHARPER THAN YA THINK!
SHCING!
HAHAHA!
AHHH!
WOOSH!
YA MAY BE SHARP, BUT YA SURE AIN'T COOL!
A LITTLE SPUR-OF-THE-MOMENT DEFENSE.
KCHINNNG
NOW I'M GETTIN' TIRED OF YOU BEIN' IN MY TOWN. AND I THINK IT'S HIGH TIME I KICK YOU OUT FOR GOOD!

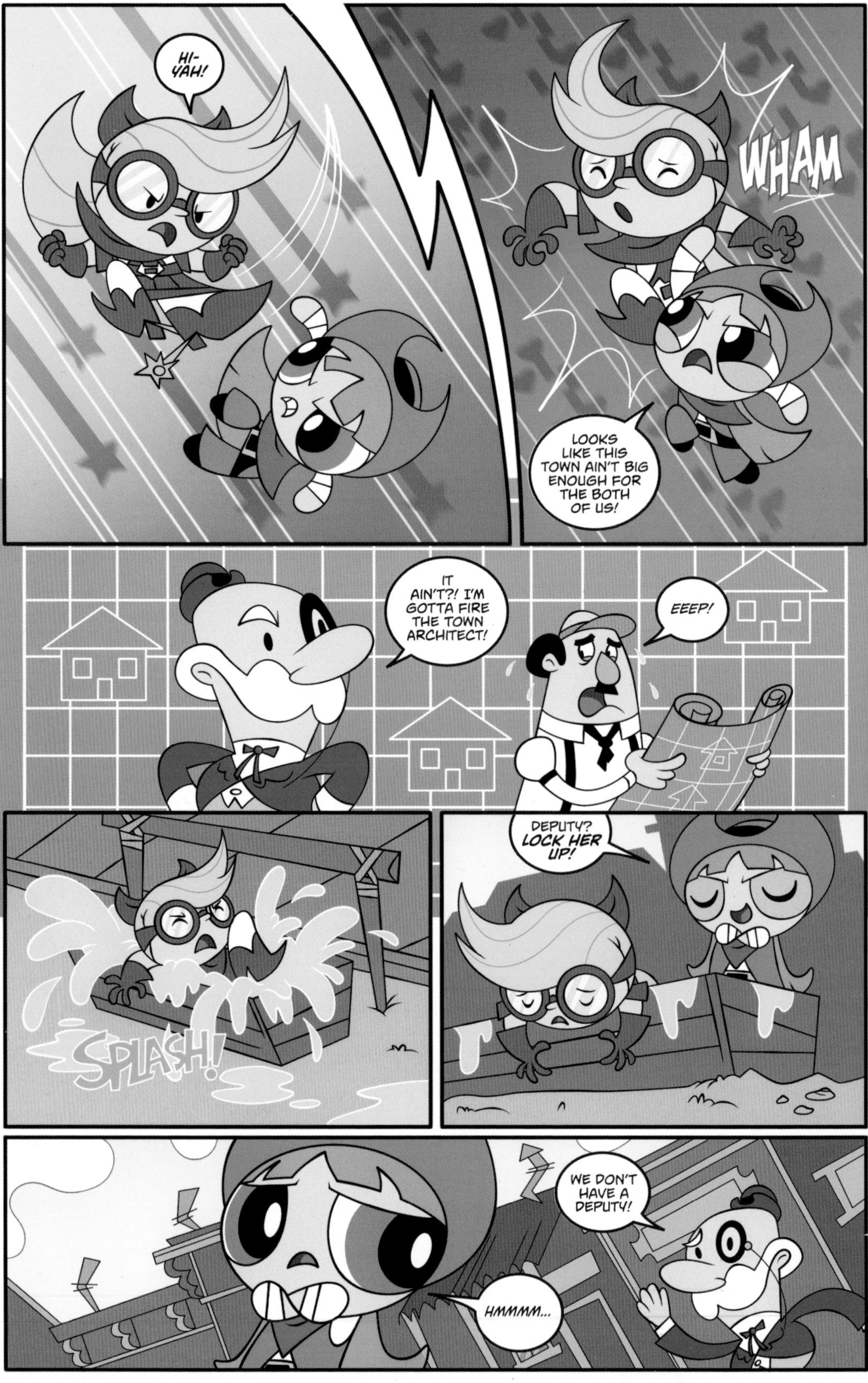
HI-YAH!
WHAM
LOOKS LIKE THIS TOWN AIN'T BIG ENOUGH FOR THE BOTH OF US!
IT AIN'T?! I'M GOTTA FIRE THE TOWN ARCHITECT!
EEEP!
SPLASH!
DEPUTY? LOCK HER UP!
WE DON'T HAVE A DEPUTY!
HMMMM...

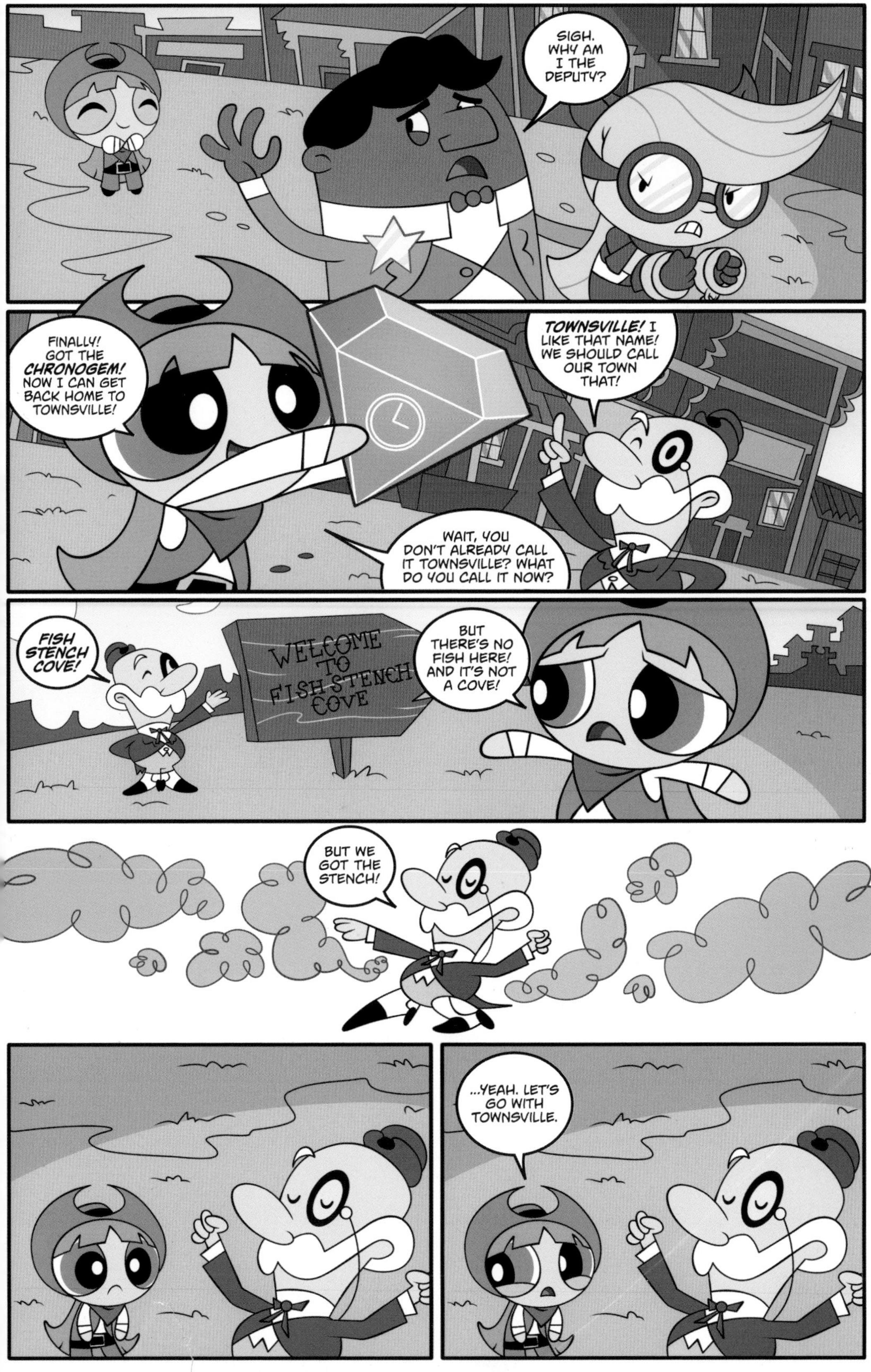
SIGH. WHY AM I THE DEPUTY?
FINALLY! GOT THE CHRONOGEM! NOW I CAN GET BACK HOME TO TOWNSVILLE!
TOWNSVILLE! I LIKE THAT NAME! WE SHOULD CALL OUR TOWN THAT!
WAIT, YOU DON'T ALREADY CALL IT TOWNSVILLE? WHAT DO YOU CALL IT NOW?
FISH STENCH COVE!
WELCOME TO FISH STENCH COVE
BUT THERE'S NO FISH HERE! AND IT'S NOT A COVE!
BUT WE GOT THE STENCH!
...YEAH. LET'S GO WITH TOWNSVILLE.

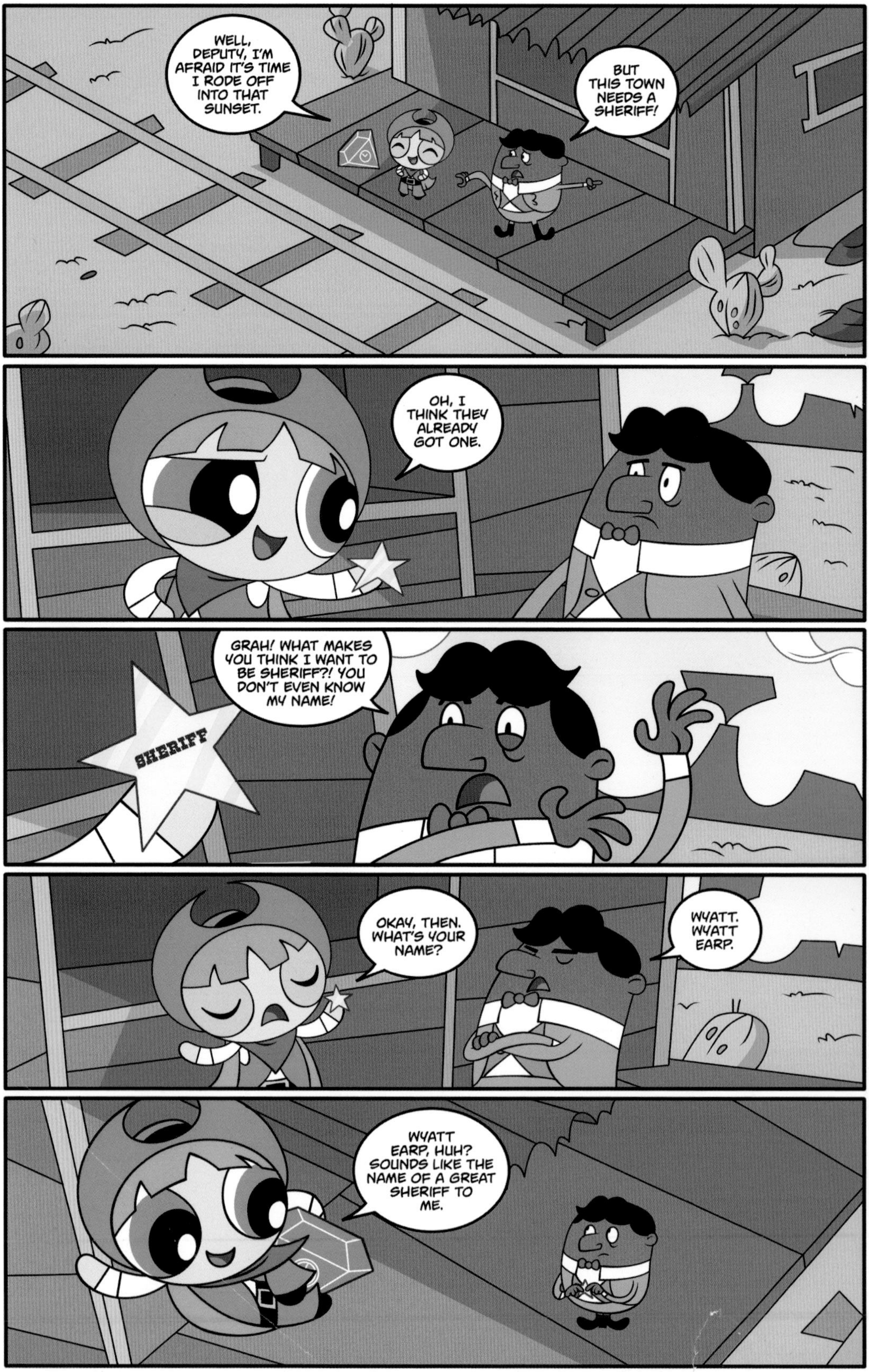
WELL, DEPUTY, I'M AFRAID IT'S TIME I RODE OFF INTO THAT SUNSET.
BUT THIS TOWN NEEDS A SHERIFF!
OH, I THINK THEY ALREADY GOT ONE.
SHERIFF
GRAH! WHAT MAKES YOU THINK I WANT TO BE SHERIFF?! YOU DON'T EVEN KNOW MY NAME!
OKAY, THEN. WHAT'S YOUR NAME?
WYATT. WYATT EARP.
WYATT EARP, HUH? SOUNDS LIKE THE NAME OF A GREAT SHERIFF TO ME.

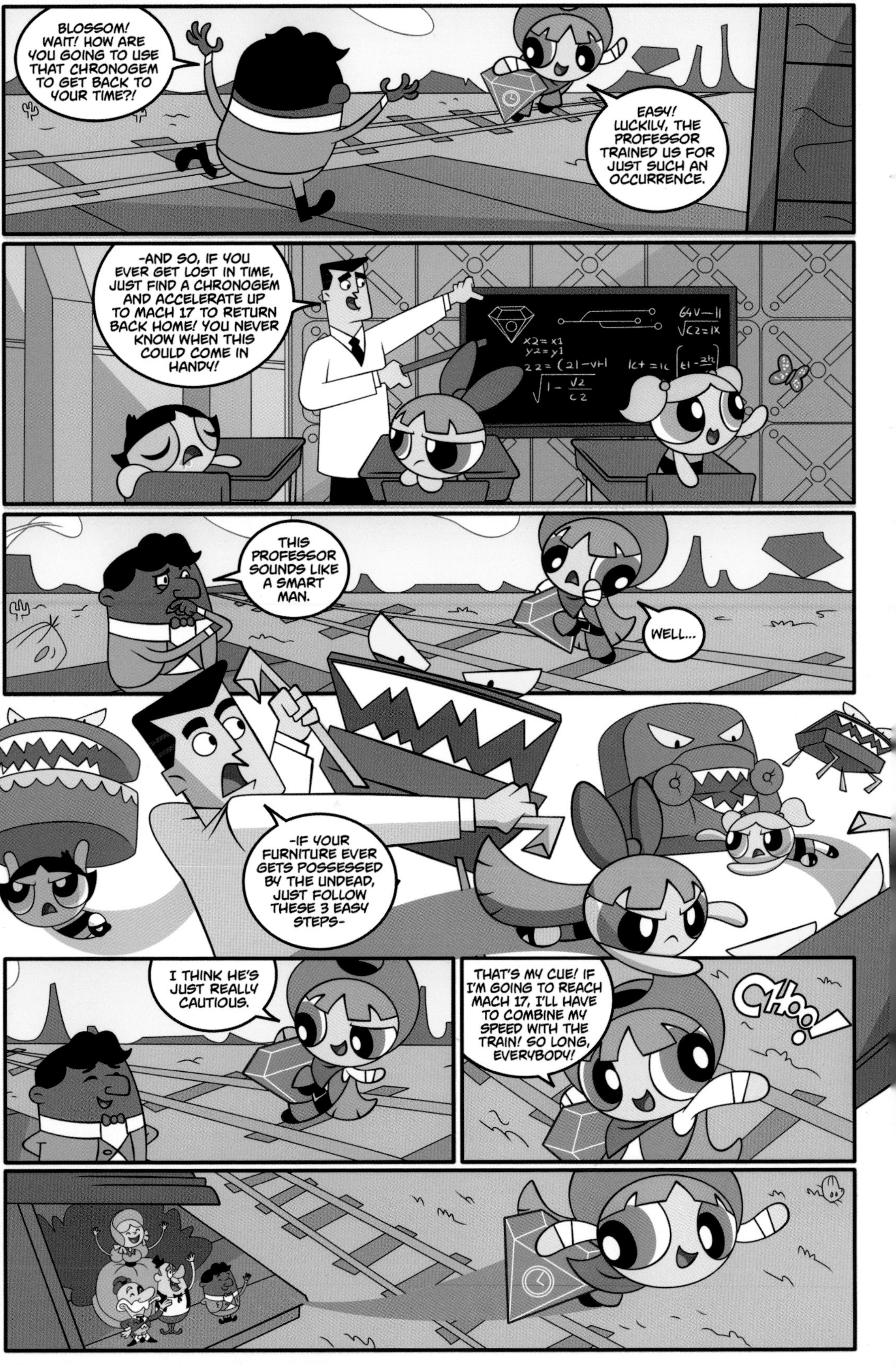

BLOSSOM! WAIT! HOW ARE YOU GOING TO USE THAT CHRONOGEM TO GET BACK TO YOUR TIME?!
EASY! LUCKILY, THE PROFESSOR TRAINED US FOR JUST SUCH AN OCCURRENCE.
-AND SO, IF YOU EVER GET LOST IN TIME, JUST FIND A CHRONOGEM AND ACCELERATE UP TO MACH 17 TO RETURN BACK HOME! YOU NEVER KNOW WHEN THIS COULD COME IN HANDY!
THIS PROFESSOR SOUNDS LIKE A SMART MAN.
WELL...
-IF YOUR FURNITURE EVER GETS POSSESSED BY THE UNDEAD, JUST FOLLOW THESE 3 EASY STEPS-
I THINK HE'S JUST REALLY CAUTIOUS.
THAT'S MY CUE! IF I'M GOING TO REACH MACH 17, I'LL HAVE TO COMBINE MY SPEED WITH THE TRAIN! SO LONG, EVERYBODY!
CHOO!

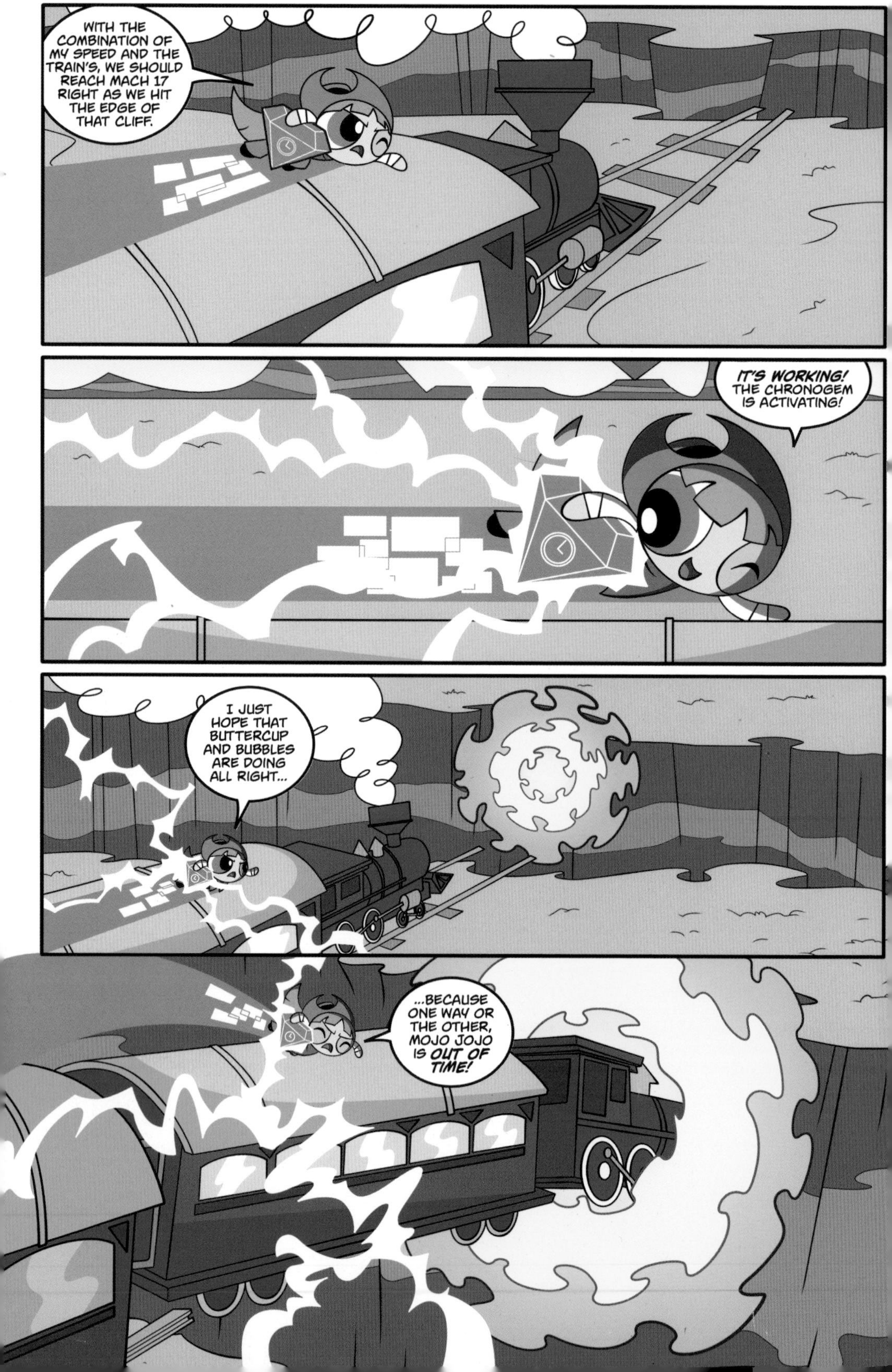
WITH THE COMBINATION OF MY SPEED AND THE TRAIN'S, WE SHOULD REACH MACH 17 RIGHT AS WE HIT THE EDGE OF THAT CLIFF.
IT'S WORKING! THE CHRONOGEM IS ACTIVATING!
I JUST HOPE THAT BUTTERCUP AND BUBBLES ARE DOING ALL RIGHT...
...BECAUSE ONE WAY OR THE OTHER, MOJO JOJO IS OUT OF TIME!

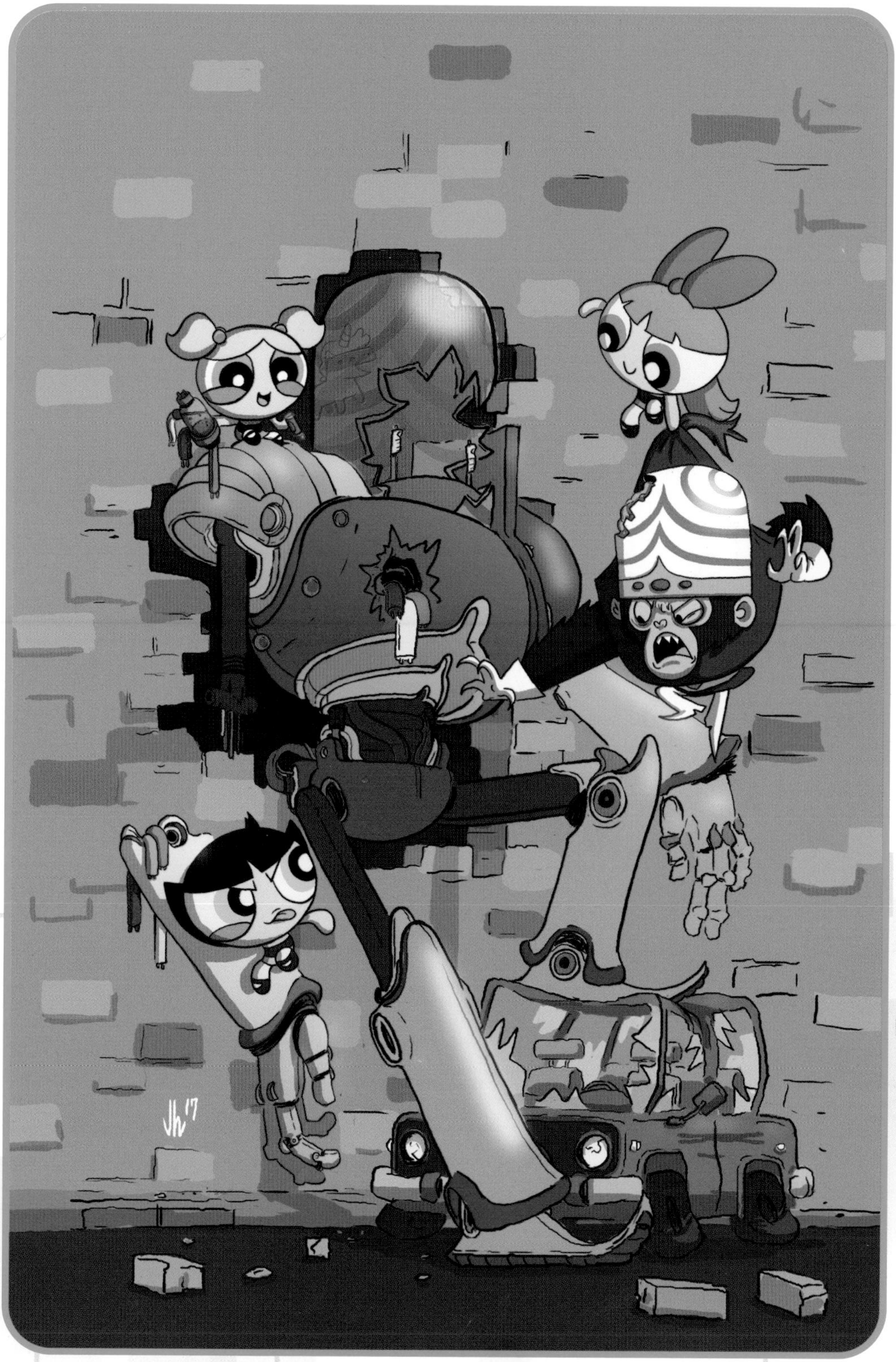
Jh'17

Cover Art by **Jay Hasrajani**

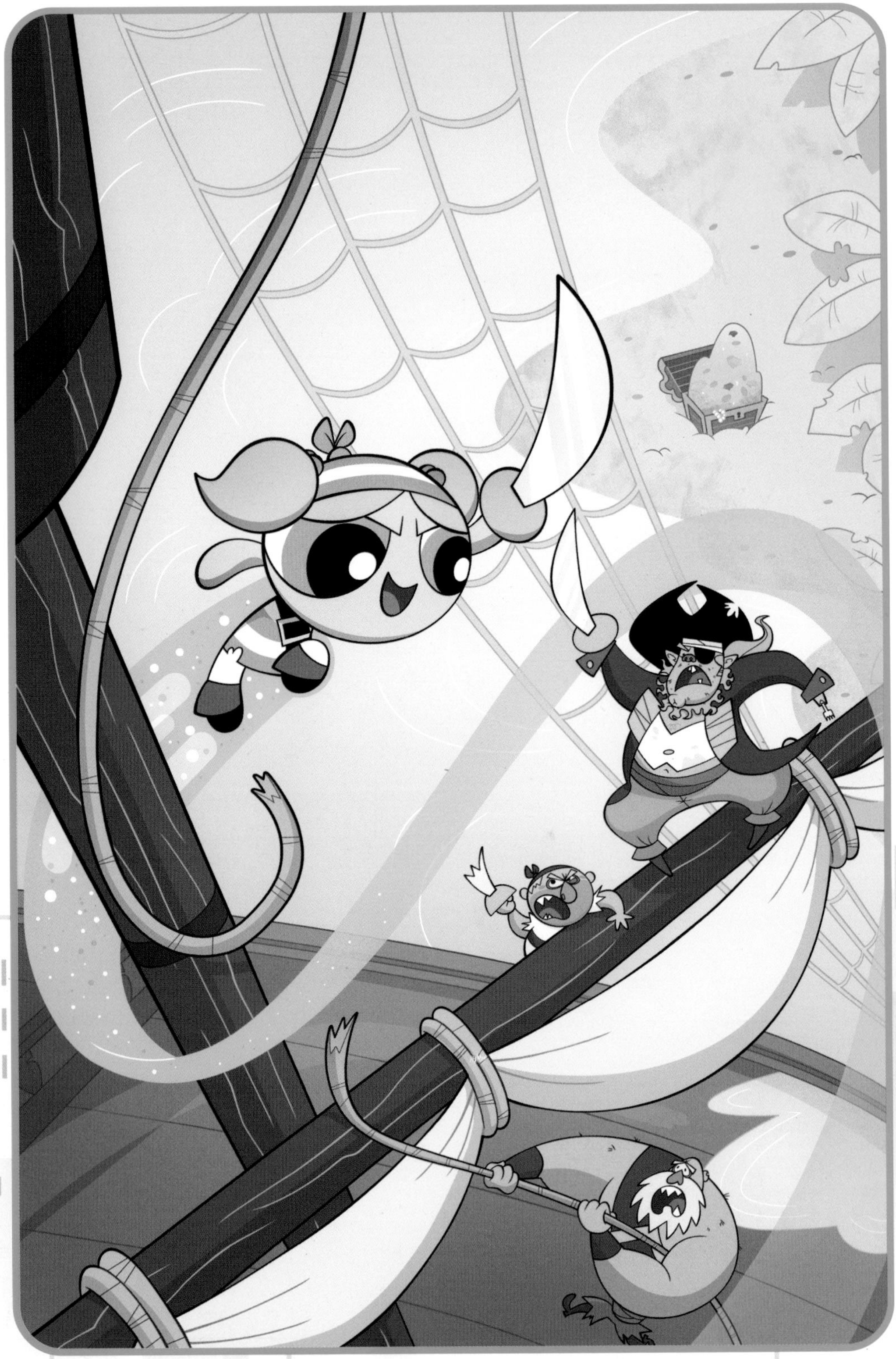

Cover Art by **Philip Murphy**

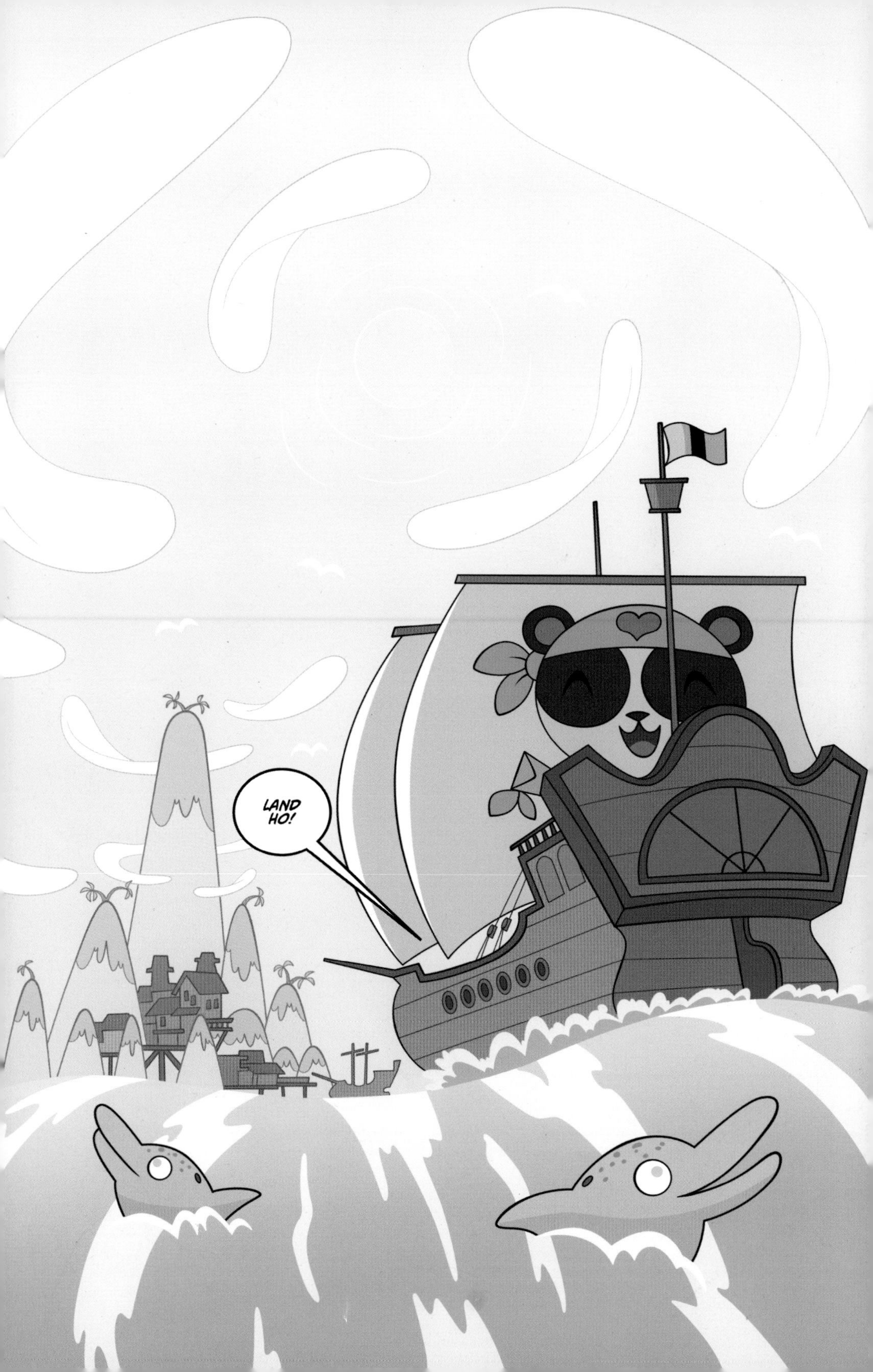
LAND HO!

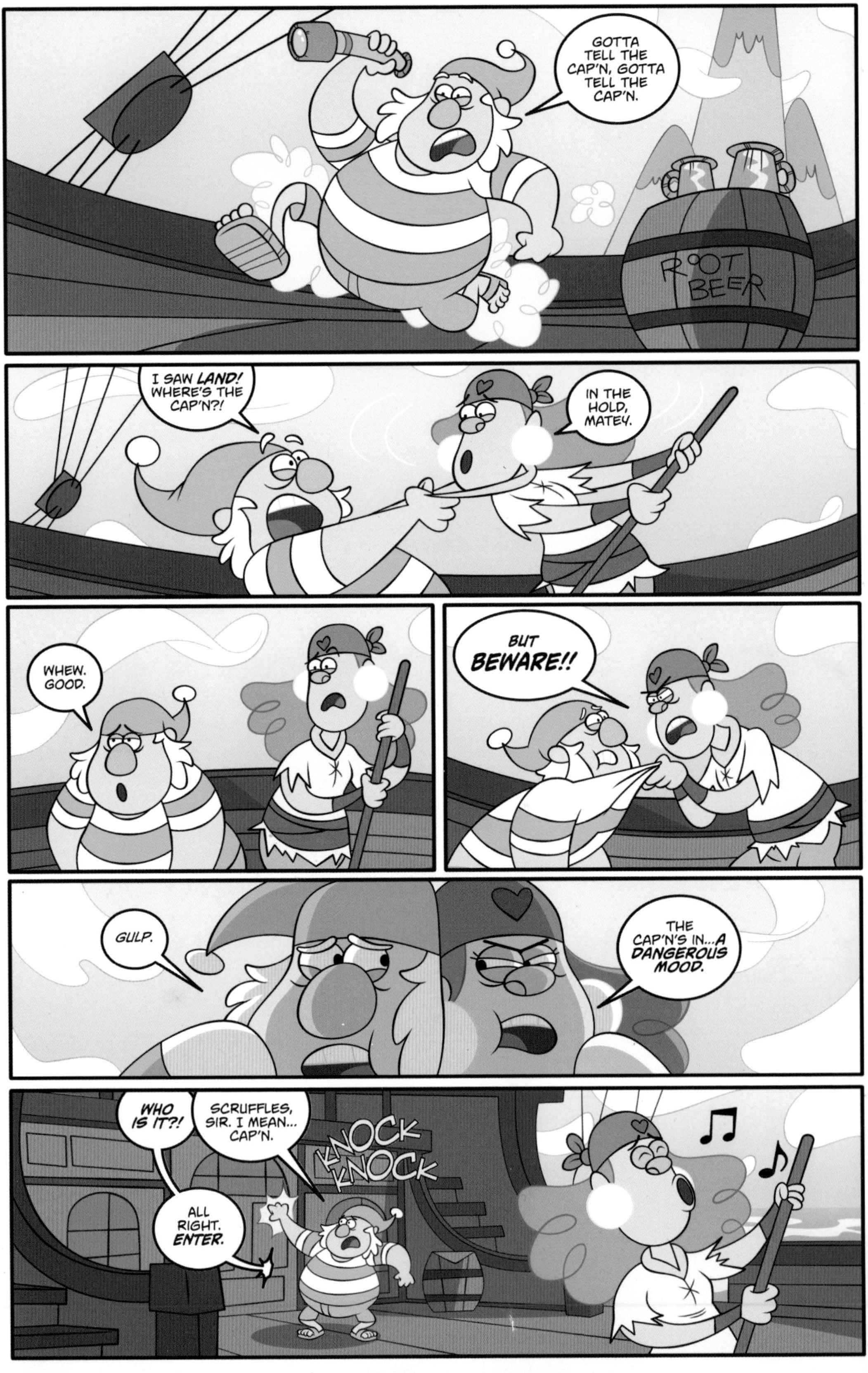
GOTTA TELL THE CAP'N, GOTTA TELL THE CAP'N.
ROOT BEER
I SAW LAND! WHERE'S THE CAP'N?!
IN THE HOLD, MATEY.
WHEW. GOOD.
BUT BEWARE!!
GULP.
THE CAP'N'S IN...A DANGEROUS MOOD.
WHO IS IT?!
SCRUFFLES, SIR. I MEAN... CAP'N.
KNOCK KNOCK
ALL RIGHT. ENTER.

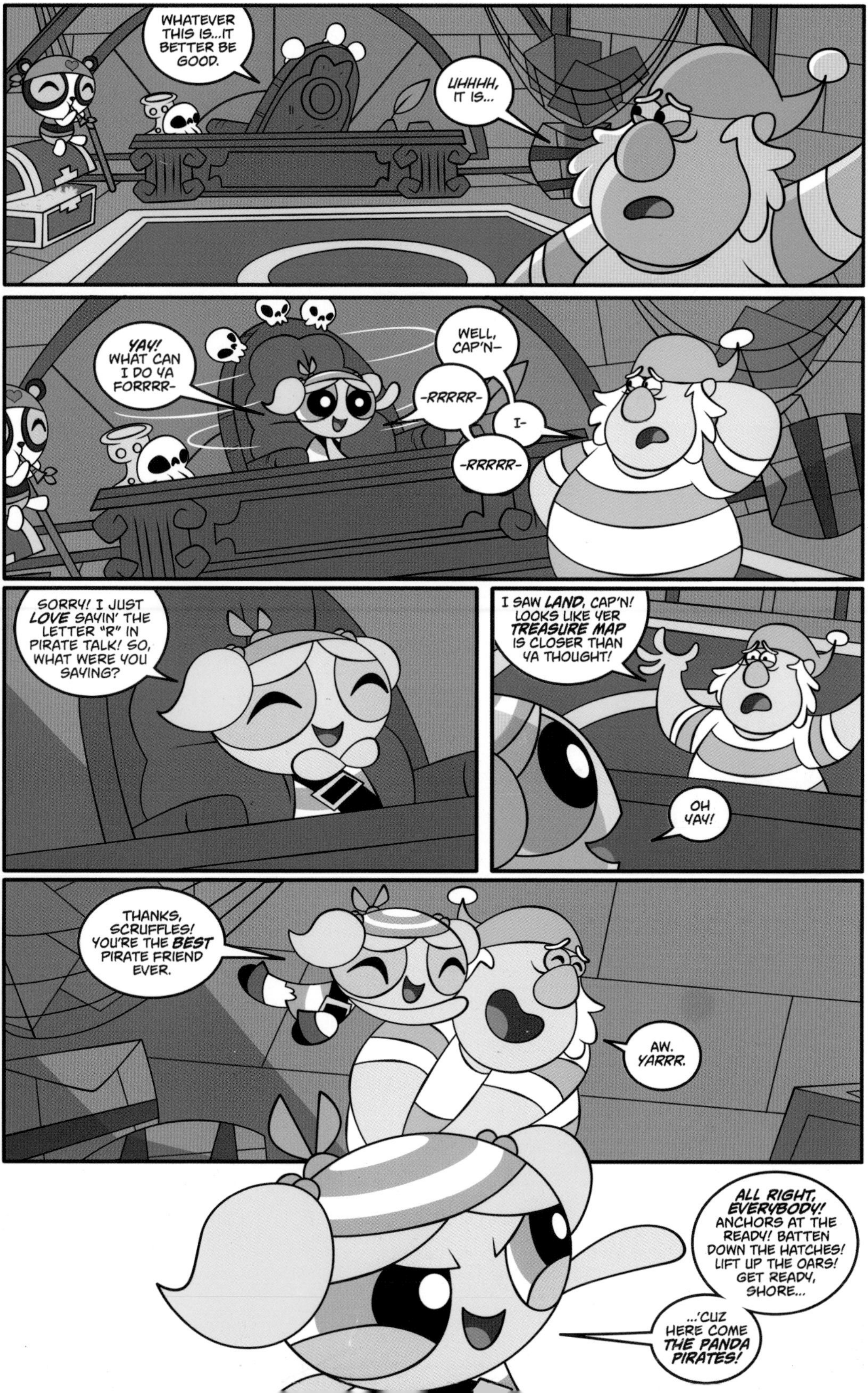
WHATEVER THIS IS...IT BETTER BE GOOD.
UHHHH, IT IS...
YAY! WHAT CAN I DO YA FORRRR-
WELL, CAP'N-
-RRRRR-
I-
-RRRRR-
SORRY! I JUST LOVE SAYIN' THE LETTER "R" IN PIRATE TALK! SO, WHAT WERE YOU SAYING?
I SAW LAND, CAP'N! LOOKS LIKE YER TREASURE MAP IS CLOSER THAN YA THOUGHT!
OH YAY!
THANKS, SCRUFFLES! YOU'RE THE BEST PIRATE FRIEND EVER.
AW. YARRR.
ALL RIGHT, EVERYBODY! ANCHORS AT THE READY! BATTEN DOWN THE HATCHES! LIFT UP THE OARS! GET READY, SHORE...
...'CUZ HERE COME THE PANDA PIRATES!

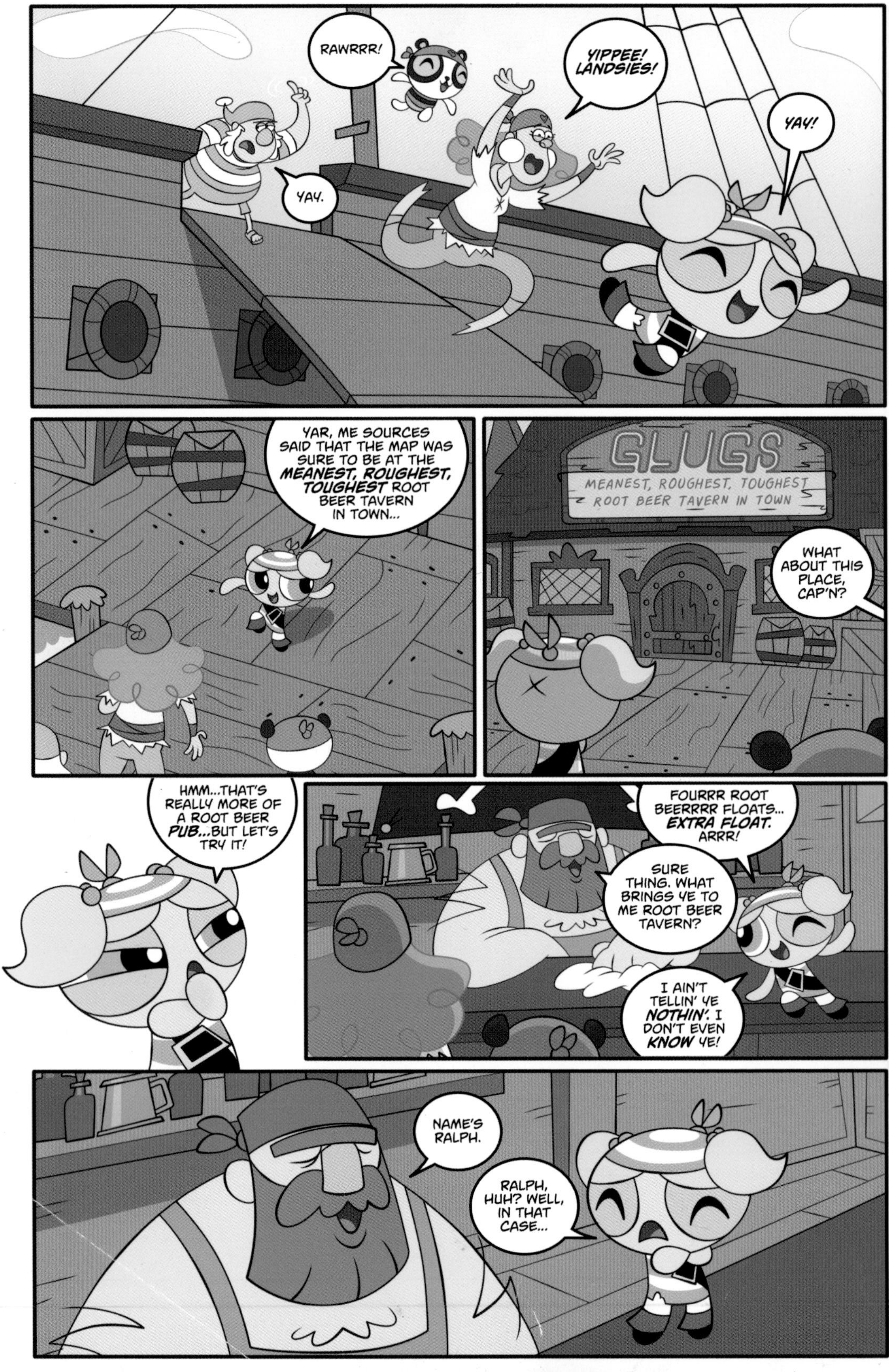

RAWRRR!
YIPPEE! LANDSIES!
YAY.
YAY!
YAR, ME SOURCES SAID THAT THE MAP WAS SURE TO BE AT THE MEANEST, ROUGHEST, TOUGHEST ROOT BEER TAVERN IN TOWN...
GLUGS
MEANEST, ROUGHEST, TOUGHEST ROOT BEER TAVERN IN TOWN
WHAT ABOUT THIS PLACE, CAP'N?
HMM...THAT'S REALLY MORE OF A ROOT BEER PUB...BUT LET'S TRY IT!
FOURRR ROOT BEERRRR FLOATS... EXTRA FLOAT. ARRR!
SURE THING. WHAT BRINGS YE TO ME ROOT BEER TAVERN?
I AIN'T TELLIN' YE NOTHIN'. I DON'T EVEN KNOW YE!
NAME'S RALPH.
RALPH, HUH? WELL, IN THAT CASE...

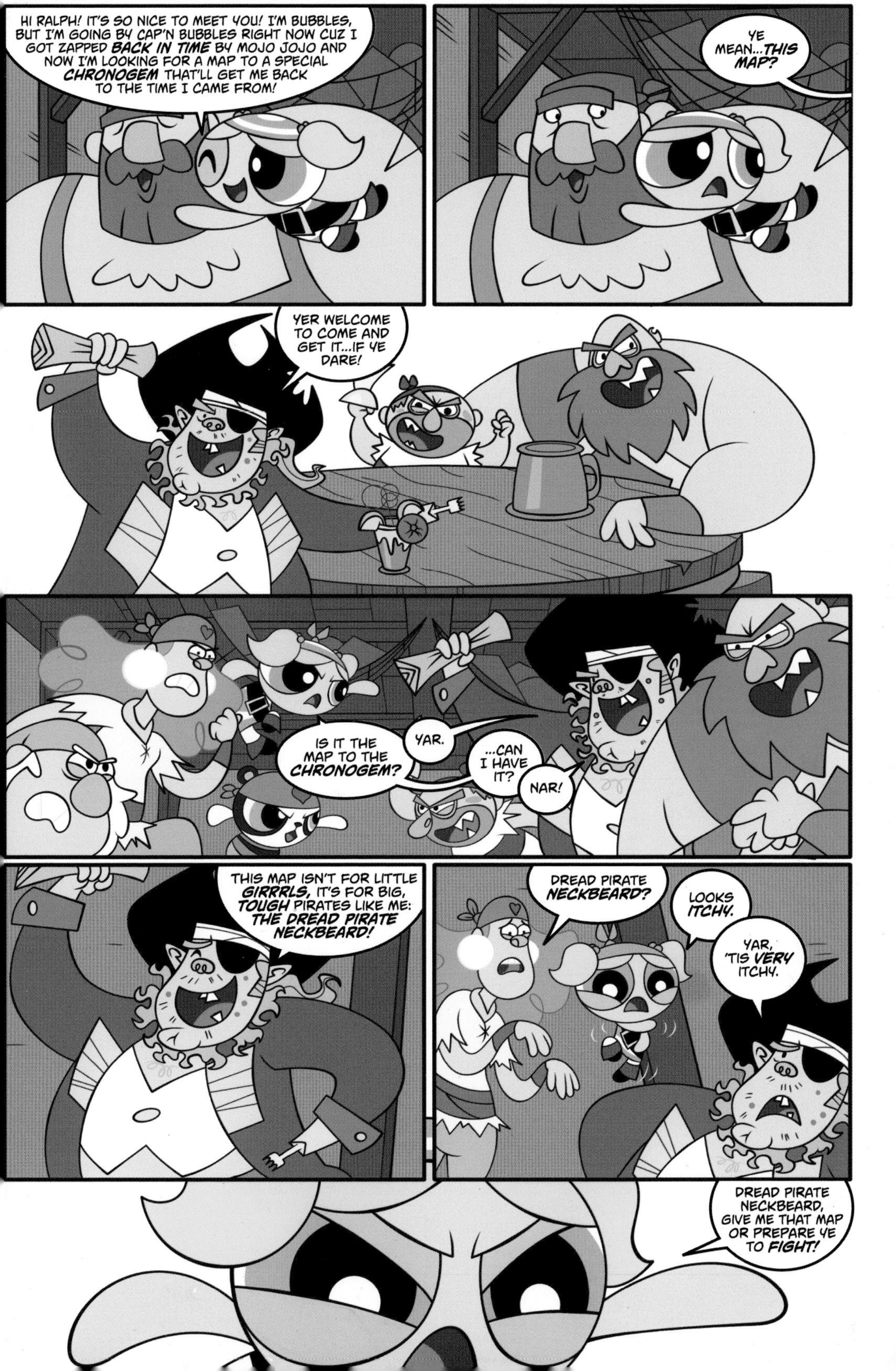

HI RALPH! IT'S SO NICE TO MEET YOU! I'M BUBBLES, BUT I'M GOING BY CAP'N BUBBLES RIGHT NOW CUZ I GOT ZAPPED BACK IN TIME BY MOJO JOJO AND NOW I'M LOOKING FOR A MAP TO A SPECIAL CHRONOGEM THAT'LL GET ME BACK TO THE TIME I CAME FROM!
YE MEAN...THIS MAP?
YER WELCOME TO COME AND GET IT...IF YE DARE!
IS IT THE MAP TO THE CHRONOGEM?
YAR.
...CAN I HAVE IT?
NAR!
THIS MAP ISN'T FOR LITTLE GIRRRLS, IT'S FOR BIG, TOUGH PIRATES LIKE ME: THE DREAD PIRATE NECKBEARD!
DREAD PIRATE NECKBEARD?
LOOKS ITCHY.
YAR, 'TIS VERY ITCHY.
DREAD PIRATE NECKBEARD, GIVE ME THAT MAP OR PREPARE YE TO FIGHT!

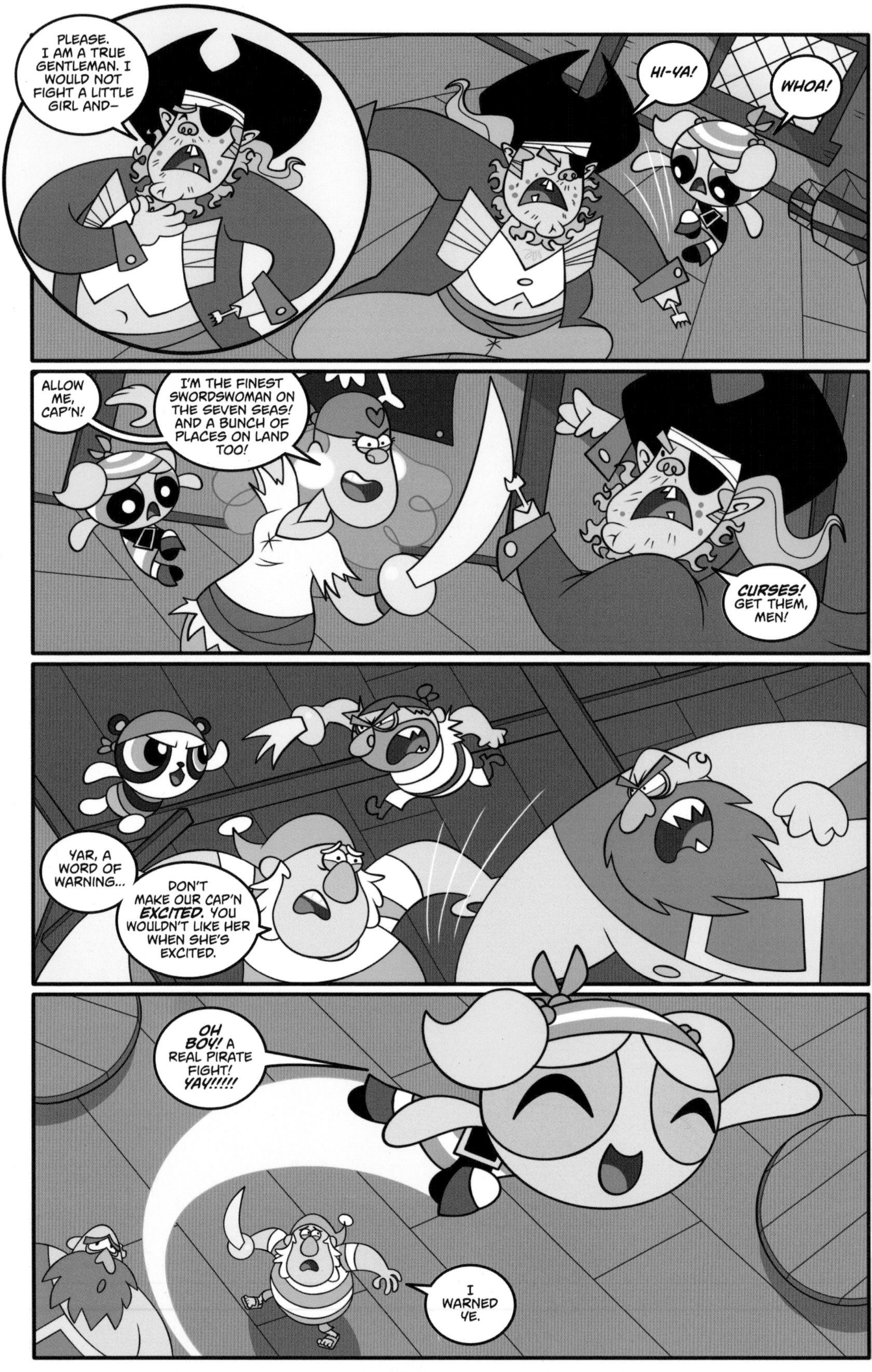
PLEASE. I AM A TRUE GENTLEMAN. I WOULD NOT FIGHT A LITTLE GIRL AND—
HI-YA!
WHOA!
ALLOW ME, CAP'N!
I'M THE FINEST SWORDSWOMAN ON THE SEVEN SEAS! AND A BUNCH OF PLACES ON LAND TOO!
CURSES! GET THEM, MEN!
YAR, A WORD OF WARNING...
DON'T MAKE OUR CAP'N EXCITED. YOU WOULDN'T LIKE HER WHEN SHE'S EXCITED.
OH BOY! A REAL PIRATE FIGHT! YAY!!!!!
I WARNED YE.

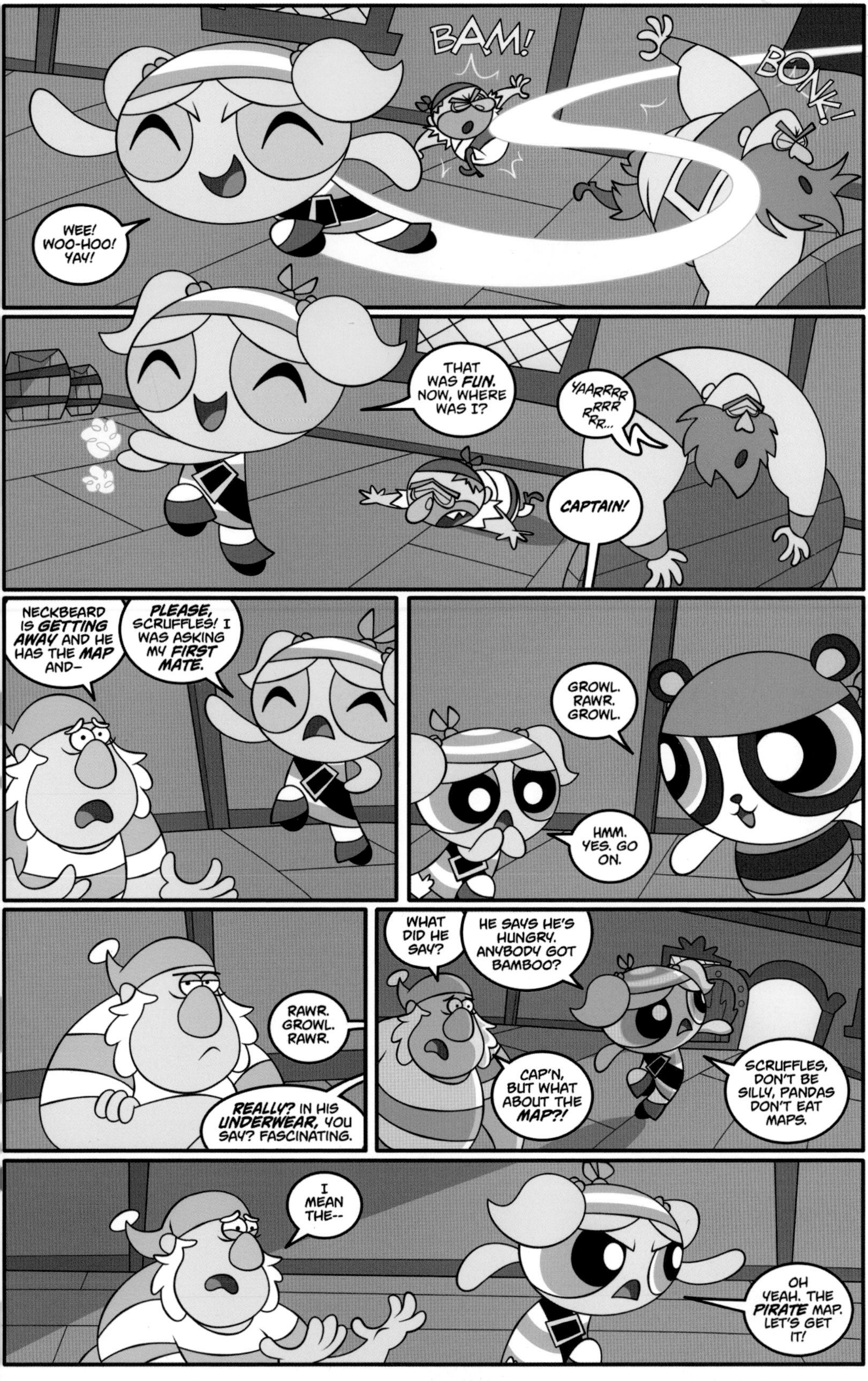
BAM!
BONK!
WEE! WOO-HOO! YAY!
THAT WAS FUN. NOW, WHERE WAS I?
YAARRRR RRRR RRR...
CAPTAIN!
NECKBEARD IS GETTING AWAY AND HE HAS THE MAP AND–
PLEASE, SCRUFFLES! I WAS ASKING MY FIRST MATE.
GROWL. RAWR. GROWL.
HMM. YES. GO ON.
RAWR. GROWL. RAWR.
REALLY? IN HIS UNDERWEAR, YOU SAY? FASCINATING.
WHAT DID HE SAY?
HE SAYS HE'S HUNGRY. ANYBODY GOT BAMBOO?
CAP'N, BUT WHAT ABOUT THE MAP?!
SCRUFFLES, DON'T BE SILLY, PANDAS DON'T EAT MAPS.
I MEAN THE--
OH YEAH. THE PIRATE MAP. LET'S GET IT!

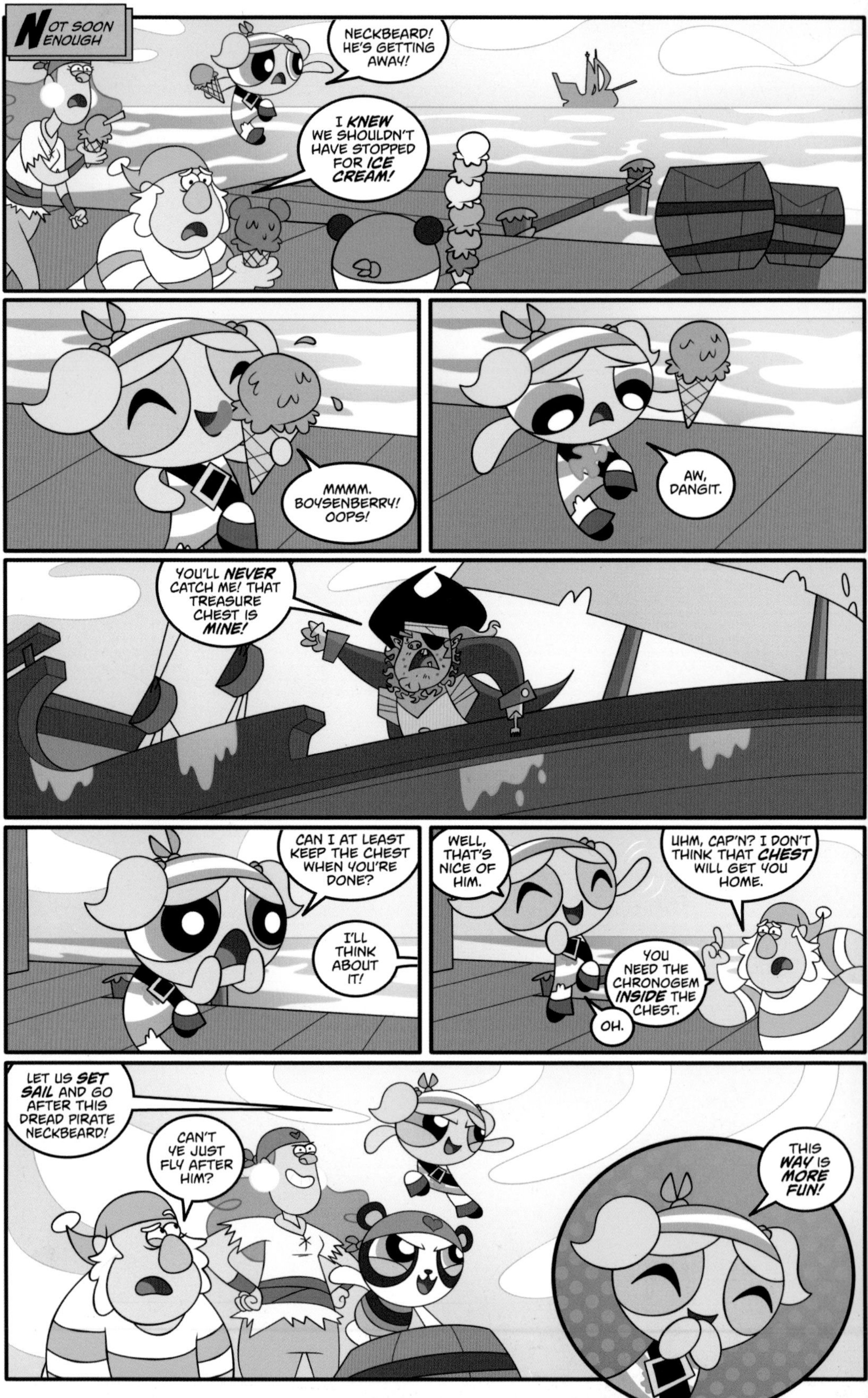
NOT SOON ENOUGH
NECKBEARD! HE'S GETTING AWAY!
I KNEW WE SHOULDN'T HAVE STOPPED FOR ICE CREAM!
MMMM. BOYSENBERRY! OOPS!
AW, DANGIT.
YOU'LL NEVER CATCH ME! THAT TREASURE CHEST IS MINE!
CAN I AT LEAST KEEP THE CHEST WHEN YOU'RE DONE?
I'LL THINK ABOUT IT!
WELL, THAT'S NICE OF HIM.
UHM, CAP'N? I DON'T THINK THAT CHEST WILL GET YOU HOME.
YOU NEED THE CHRONOGEM INSIDE THE CHEST.
OH.
LET US SET SAIL AND GO AFTER THIS DREAD PIRATE NECKBEARD!
CAN'T YE JUST FLY AFTER HIM?
THIS WAY IS MORE FUN!

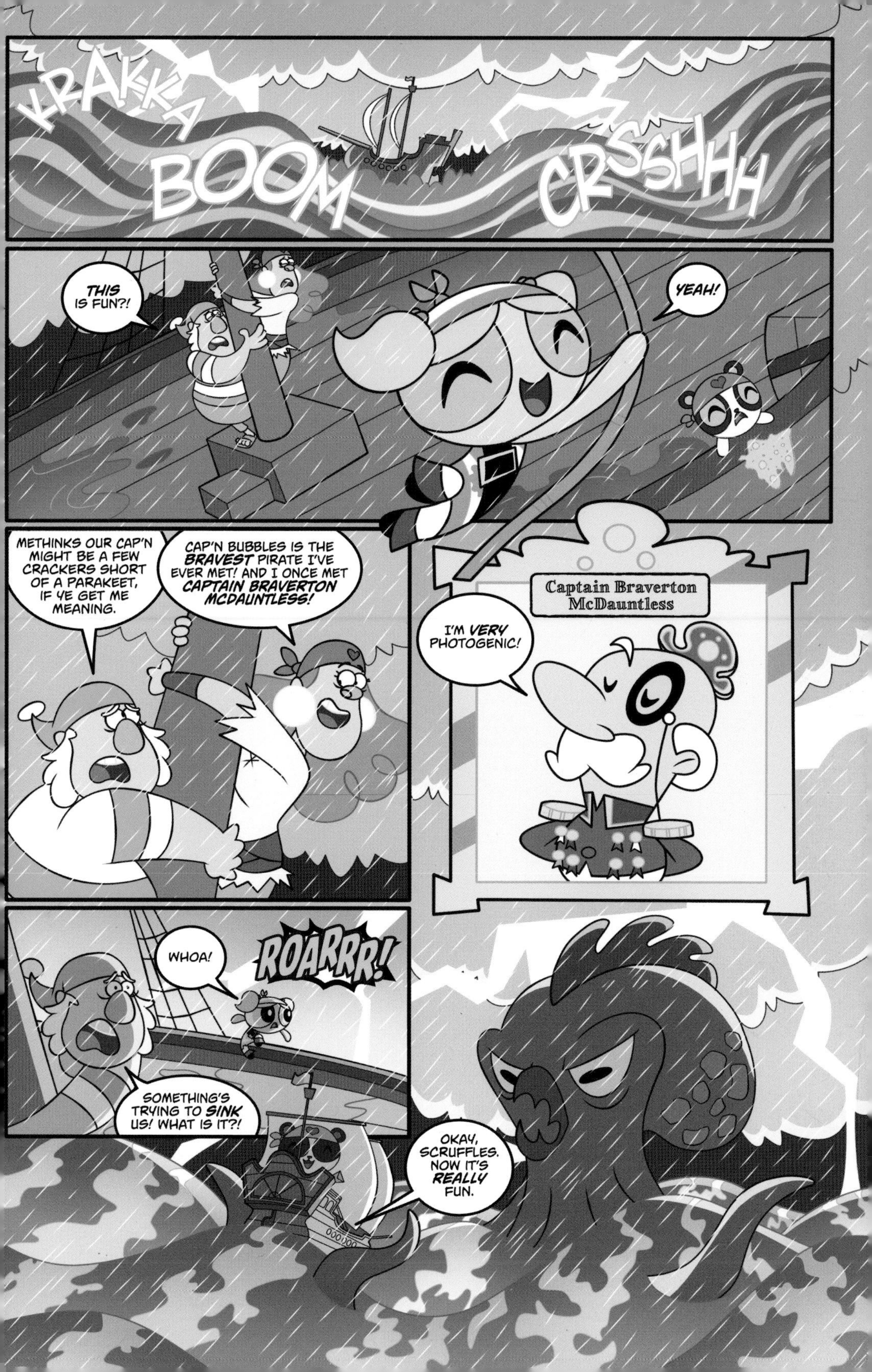
KRAKKA
BOOM
CRSSHHH
THIS IS FUN?!
YEAH!
METHINKS OUR CAP'N MIGHT BE A FEW CRACKERS SHORT OF A PARAKEET, IF YE GET ME MEANING.
CAP'N BUBBLES IS THE BRAVEST PIRATE I'VE EVER MET! AND I ONCE MET CAPTAIN BRAVERTON MCDAUNTLESS!
Captain Braverton McDauntless
I'M VERY PHOTOGENIC!
WHOA!
ROARRR!
SOMETHING'S TRYING TO SINK US! WHAT IS IT?!
OKAY, SCRUFFLES. NOW IT'S REALLY FUN.

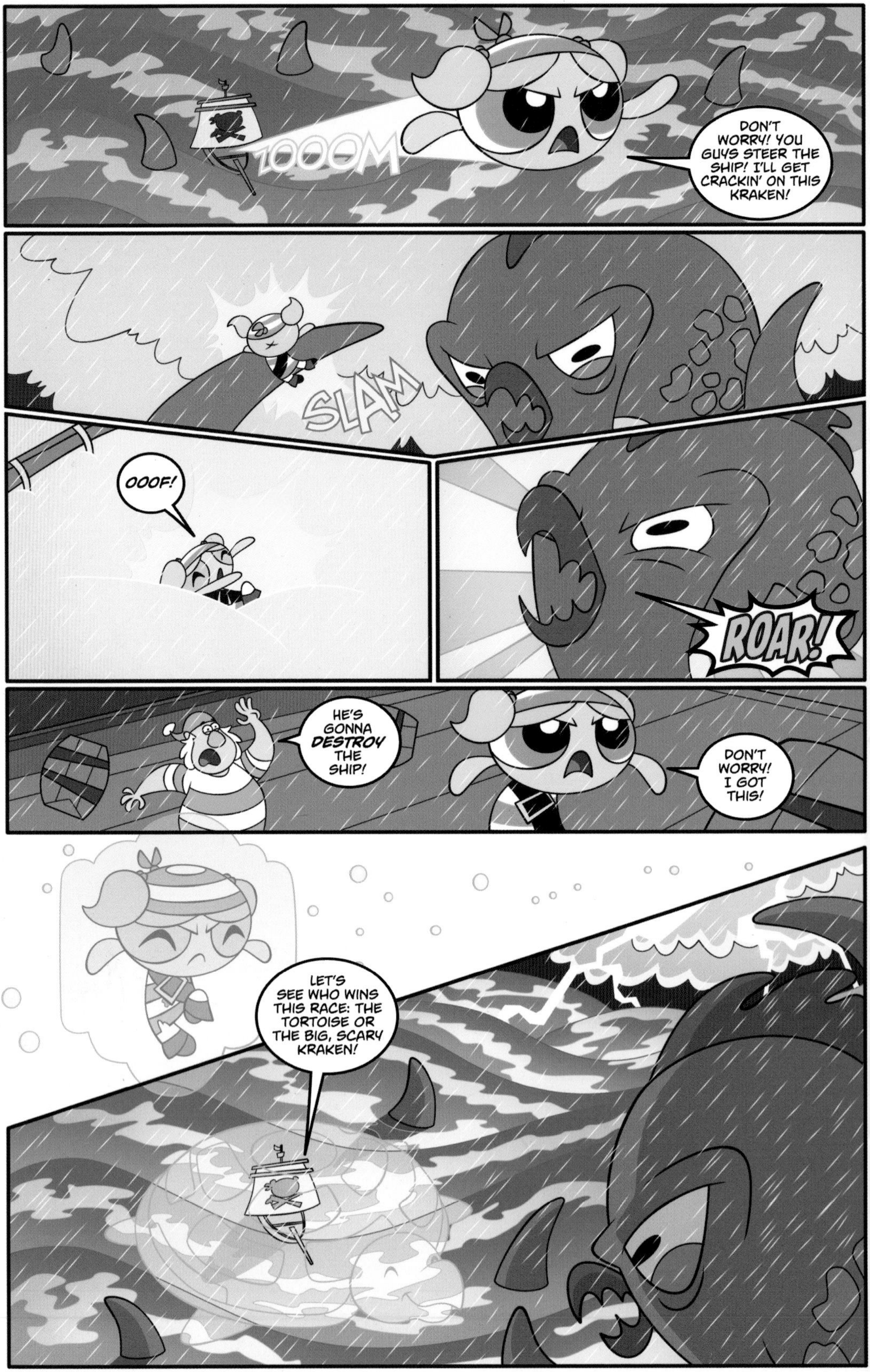
ZOOOM
DON'T WORRY! YOU GUYS STEER THE SHIP! I'LL GET CRACKIN' ON THIS KRAKEN!
SLAM
OOOF!
ROAR!
HE'S GONNA DESTROY THE SHIP!
DON'T WORRY! I GOT THIS!
LET'S SEE WHO WINS THIS RACE: THE TORTOISE OR THE BIG, SCARY KRAKEN!

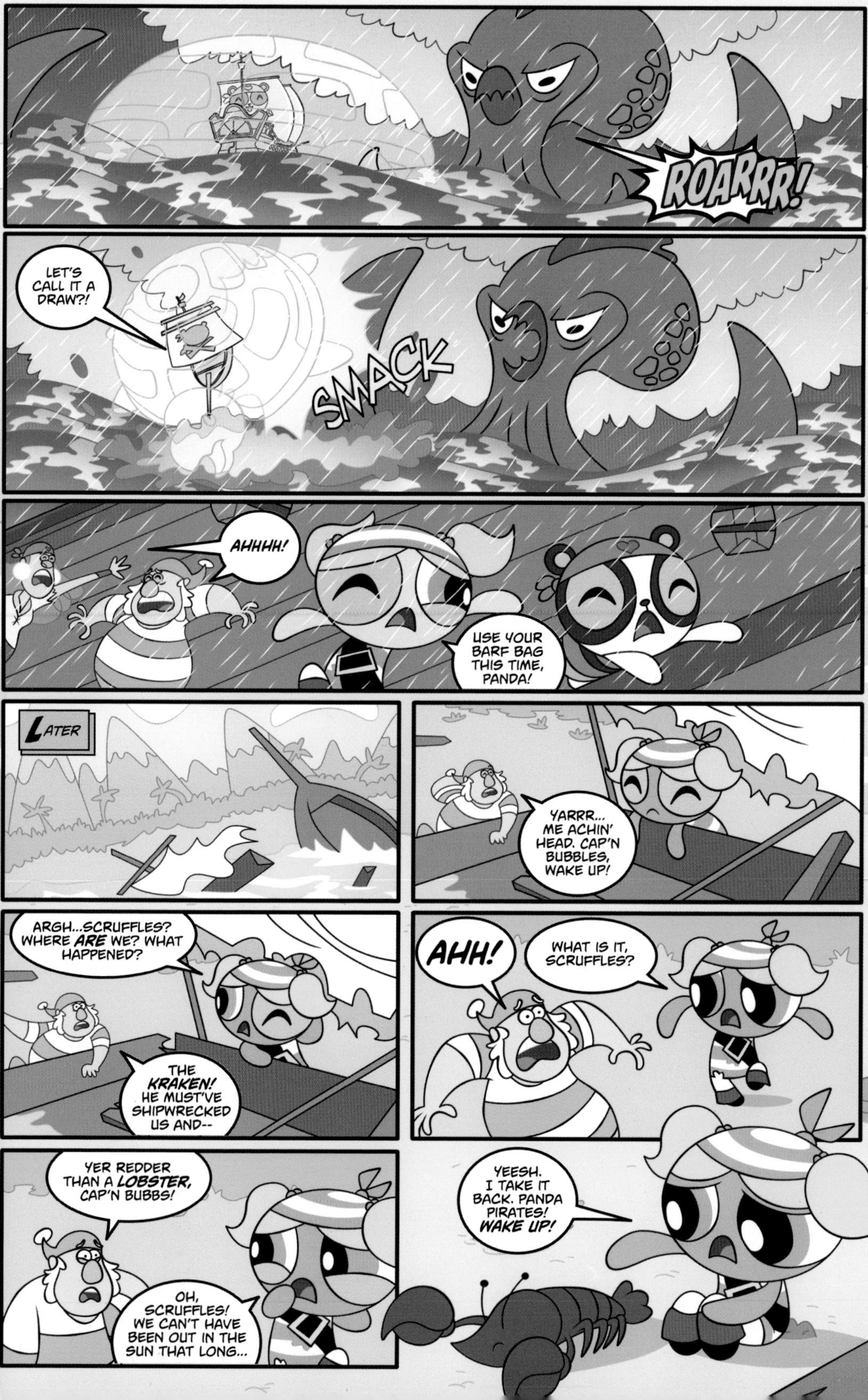
ROARRR!
LET'S CALL IT A DRAW?!
SMACK
AHHHH!
USE YOUR BARF BAG THIS TIME, PANDA!
LATER
YARRR... ME ACHIN' HEAD. CAP'N BUBBLES, WAKE UP!
ARGH...SCRUFFLES? WHERE ARE WE? WHAT HAPPENED?
THE KRAKEN! HE MUST'VE SHIPWRECKED US AND--
AHH!
WHAT IS IT, SCRUFFLES?
YER REDDER THAN A LOBSTER, CAP'N BUBBS!
OH, SCRUFFLES! WE CAN'T HAVE BEEN OUT IN THE SUN THAT LONG...
YEESH. I TAKE IT BACK. PANDA PIRATES! WAKE UP!

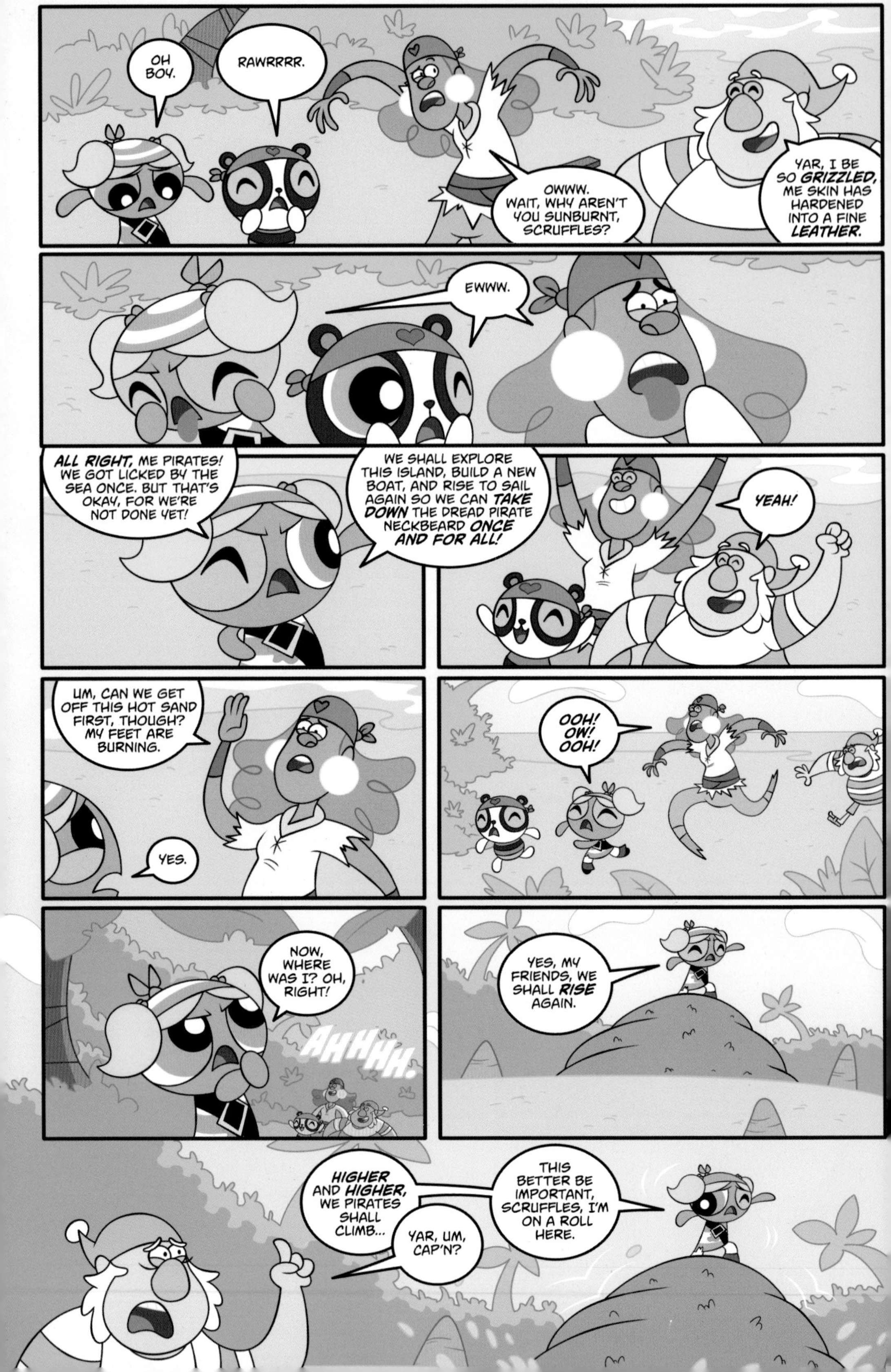
OH BOY.
RAWRRRR.
OWWW. WAIT, WHY AREN'T YOU SUNBURNT, SCRUFFLES?
YAR, I BE SO GRIZZLED, ME SKIN HAS HARDENED INTO A FINE LEATHER.
EWWW.
ALL RIGHT, ME PIRATES! WE GOT LICKED BY THE SEA ONCE. BUT THAT'S OKAY, FOR WE'RE NOT DONE YET!
WE SHALL EXPLORE THIS ISLAND, BUILD A NEW BOAT, AND RISE TO SAIL AGAIN SO WE CAN TAKE DOWN THE DREAD PIRATE NECKBEARD ONCE AND FOR ALL!
YEAH!
UM, CAN WE GET OFF THIS HOT SAND FIRST, THOUGH? MY FEET ARE BURNING.
YES.
OOH! OW! OOH!
NOW, WHERE WAS I? OH, RIGHT!
AHHHH.
YES, MY FRIENDS, WE SHALL RISE AGAIN.
HIGHER AND HIGHER, WE PIRATES SHALL CLIMB...
YAR, UM, CAP'N?
THIS BETTER BE IMPORTANT, SCRUFFLES, I'M ON A ROLL HERE.

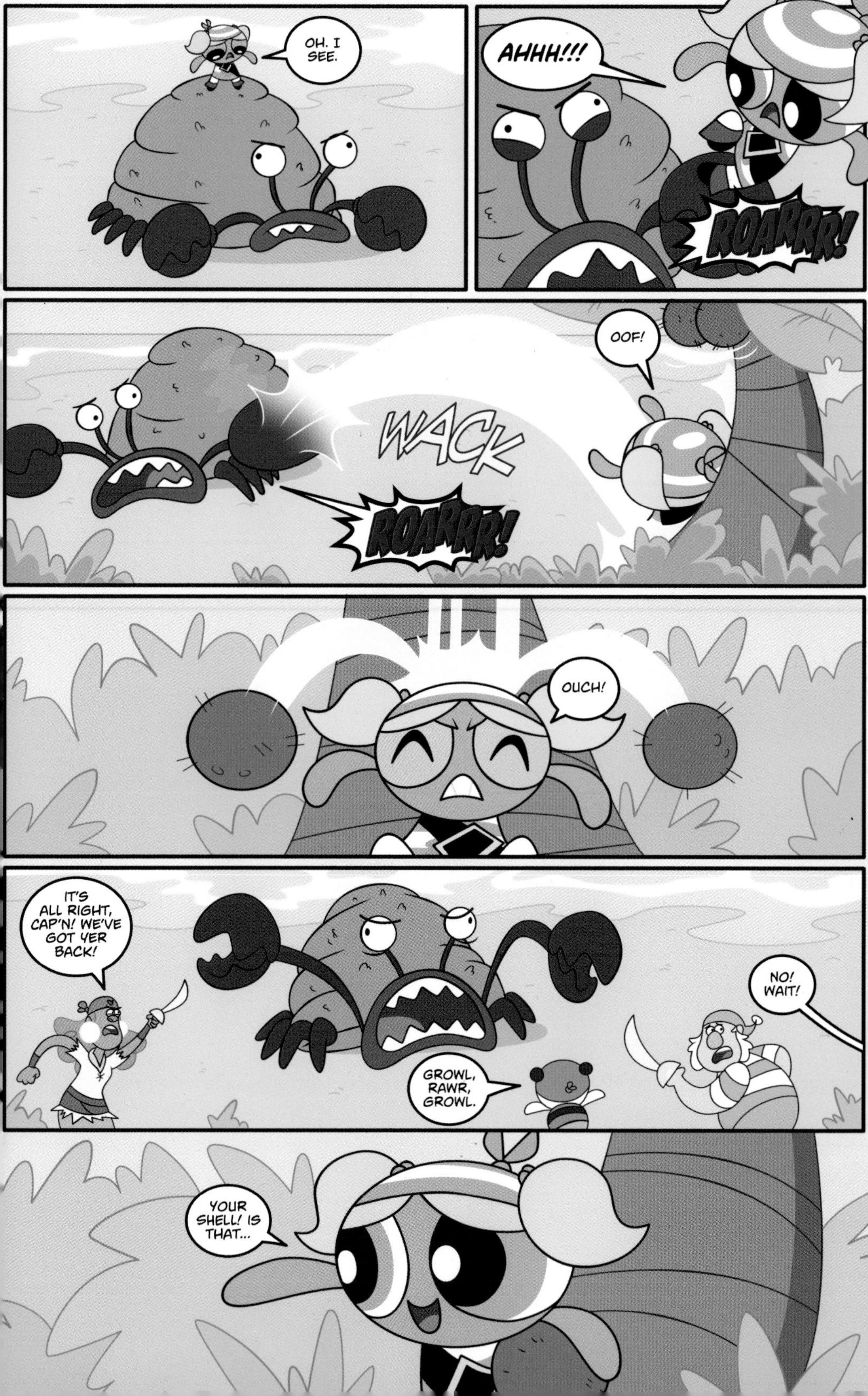
OH. I SEE.
AHHH!!!
ROARRR!
OOF!
WACK
ROARRR!
OUCH!
IT'S ALL RIGHT, CAP'N! WE'VE GOT YER BACK!
NO! WAIT!
GROWL, RAWR, GROWL.
YOUR SHELL! IS THAT...

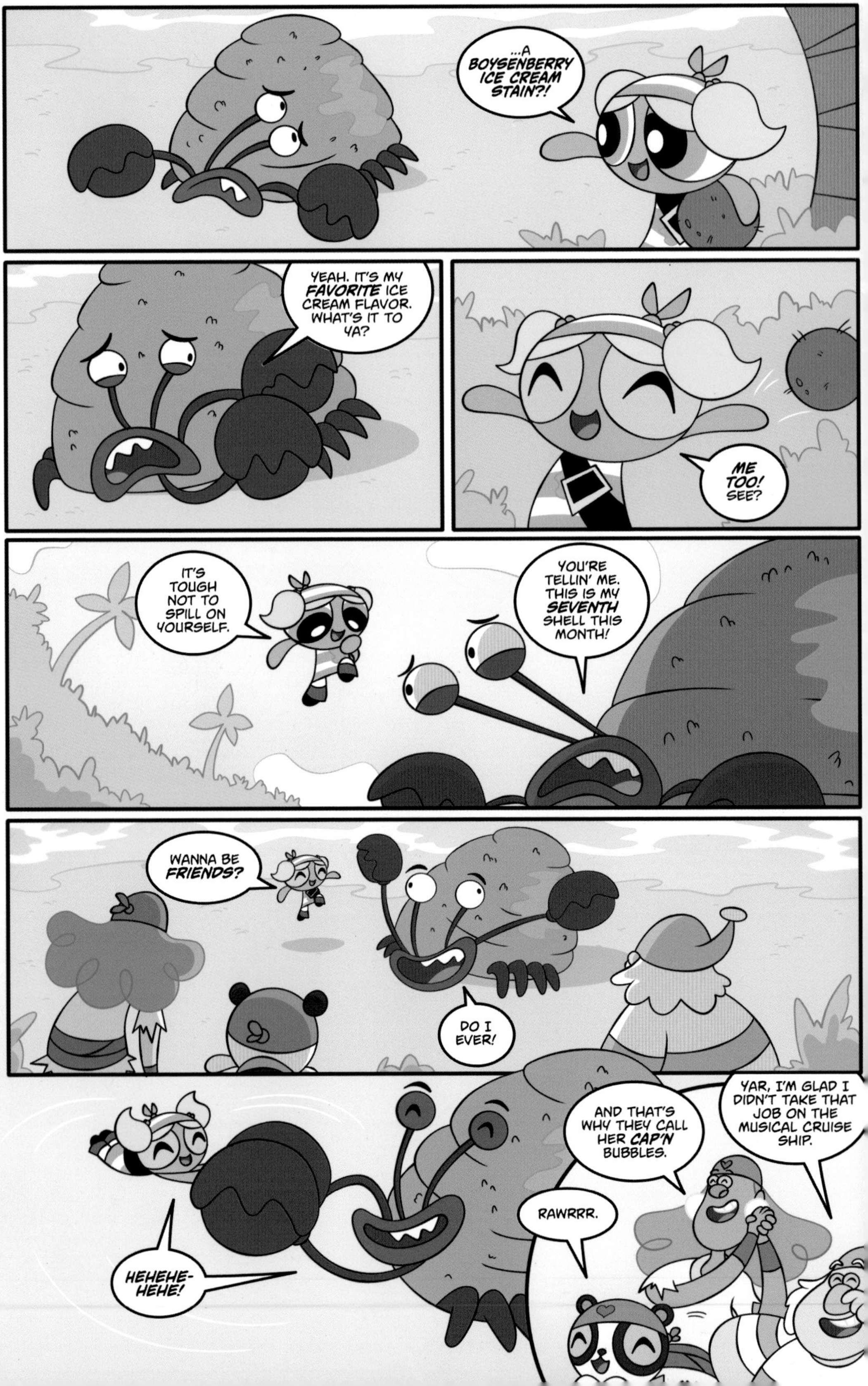
...A BOYSENBERRY ICE CREAM STAIN?!
YEAH. IT'S MY FAVORITE ICE CREAM FLAVOR. WHAT'S IT TO YA?
ME TOO! SEE?
IT'S TOUGH NOT TO SPILL ON YOURSELF.
YOU'RE TELLIN' ME. THIS IS MY SEVENTH SHELL THIS MONTH!
WANNA BE FRIENDS?
DO I EVER!
YAR, I'M GLAD I DIDN'T TAKE THAT JOB ON THE MUSICAL CRUISE SHIP.
AND THAT'S WHY THEY CALL HER CAP'N BUBBLES.
RAWRRR.
HEHEHE-HEHE!

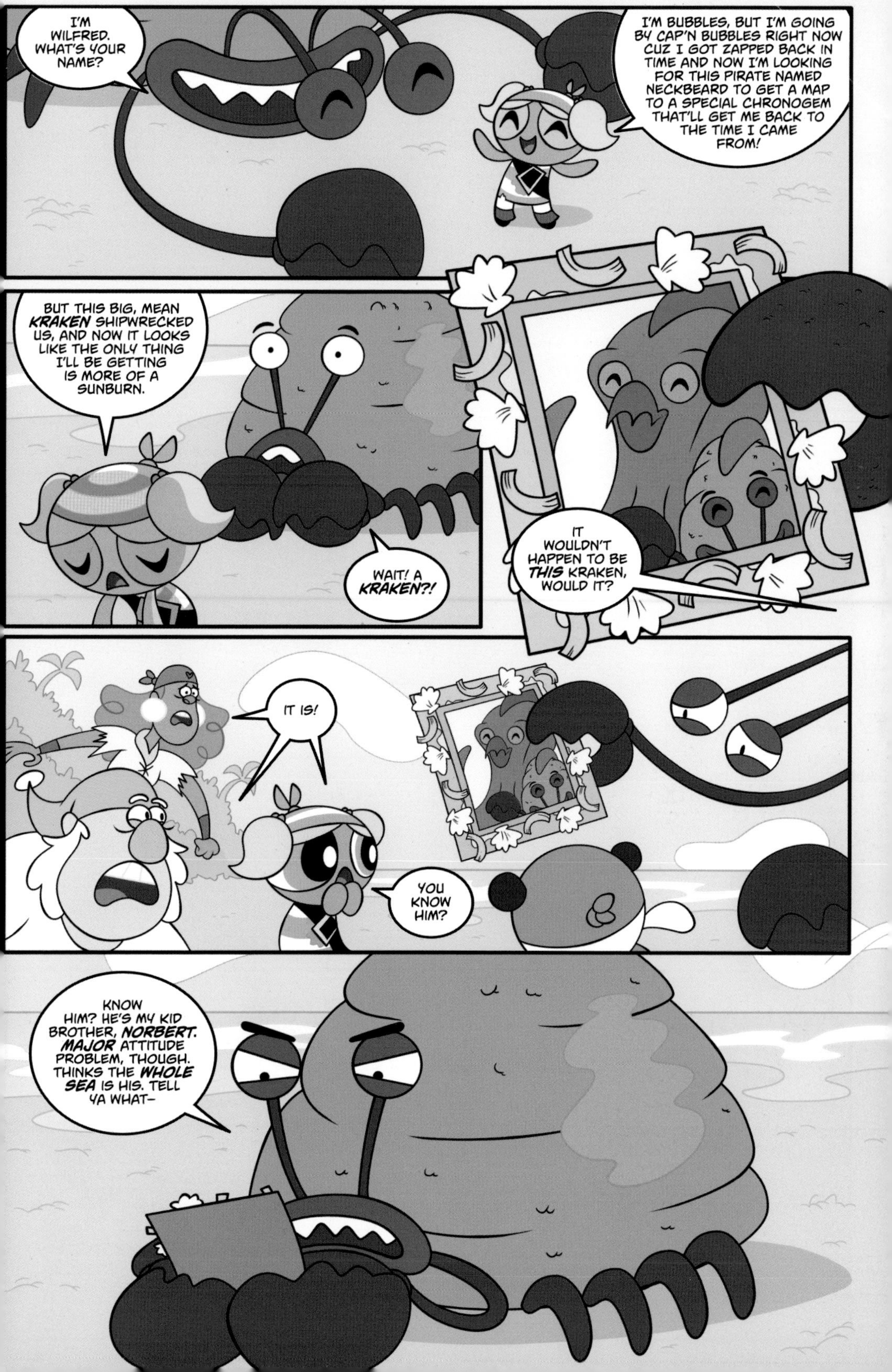

I'M WILFRED. WHAT'S YOUR NAME?
I'M BUBBLES, BUT I'M GOING BY CAP'N BUBBLES RIGHT NOW CUZ I GOT ZAPPED BACK IN TIME AND NOW I'M LOOKING FOR THIS PIRATE NAMED NECKBEARD TO GET A MAP TO A SPECIAL CHRONOGEM THAT'LL GET ME BACK TO THE TIME I CAME FROM!
BUT THIS BIG, MEAN KRAKEN SHIPWRECKED US, AND NOW IT LOOKS LIKE THE ONLY THING I'LL BE GETTING IS MORE OF A SUNBURN.
WAIT! A KRAKEN?!
IT WOULDN'T HAPPEN TO BE THIS KRAKEN, WOULD IT?
IT IS!
YOU KNOW HIM?
KNOW HIM? HE'S MY KID BROTHER, NORBERT. MAJOR ATTITUDE PROBLEM, THOUGH. THINKS THE WHOLE SEA IS HIS. TELL YA WHAT–

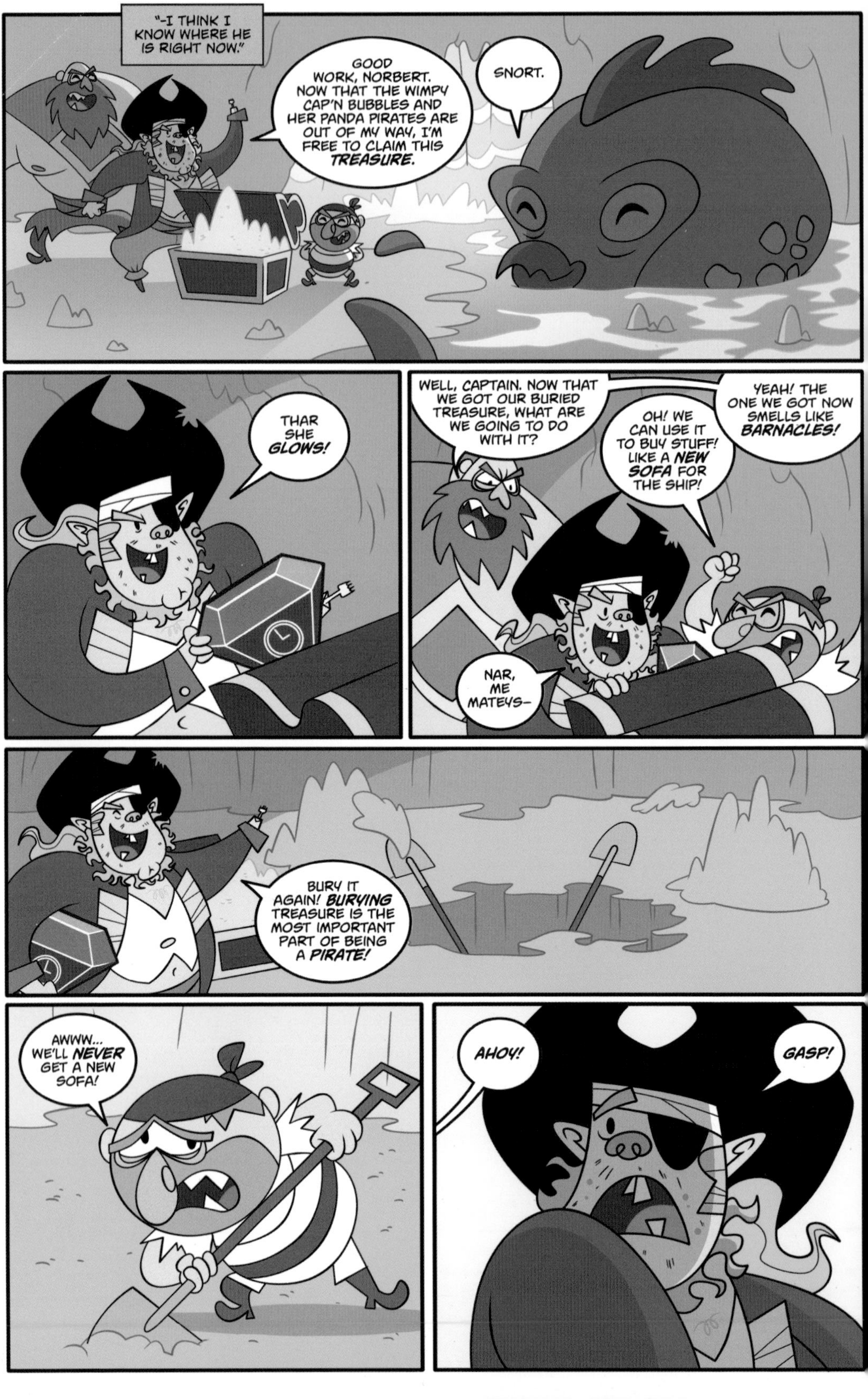
"–I THINK I KNOW WHERE HE IS RIGHT NOW."
GOOD WORK, NORBERT. NOW THAT THE WIMPY CAP'N BUBBLES AND HER PANDA PIRATES ARE OUT OF MY WAY, I'M FREE TO CLAIM THIS TREASURE.
SNORT.
THAR SHE GLOWS!
WELL, CAPTAIN. NOW THAT WE GOT OUR BURIED TREASURE, WHAT ARE WE GOING TO DO WITH IT?
OH! WE CAN USE IT TO BUY STUFF! LIKE A NEW SOFA FOR THE SHIP!
YEAH! THE ONE WE GOT NOW SMELLS LIKE BARNACLES!
NAR, ME MATEYS–
BURY IT AGAIN! BURYING TREASURE IS THE MOST IMPORTANT PART OF BEING A PIRATE!
AWWW... WE'LL NEVER GET A NEW SOFA!
AHOY!
GASP!

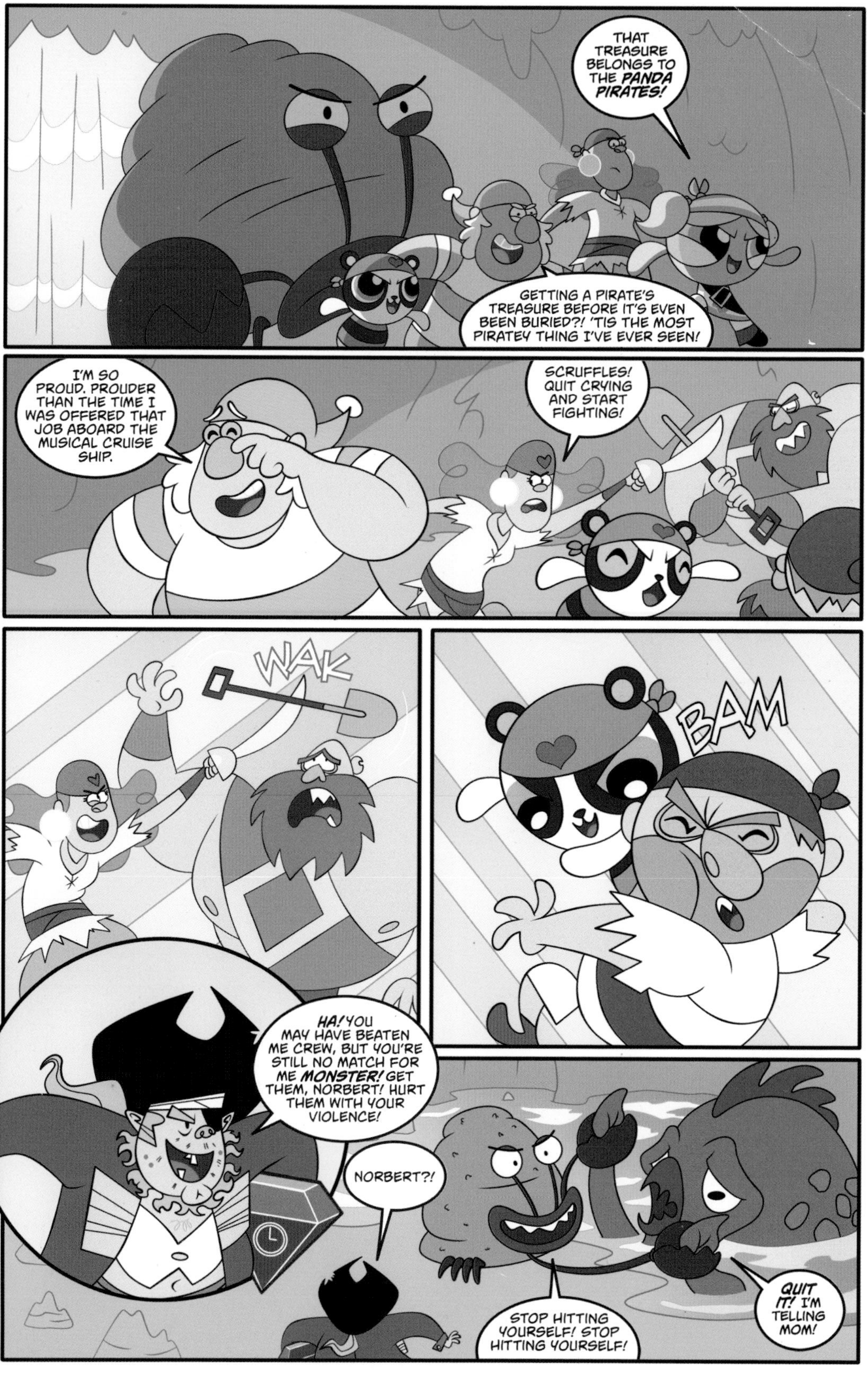

THAT TREASURE BELONGS TO THE *PANDA PIRATES!*
GETTING A PIRATE'S TREASURE BEFORE IT'S EVEN BEEN BURIED?! 'TIS THE MOST PIRATEY THING I'VE EVER SEEN!
I'M SO PROUD. PROUDER THAN THE TIME I WAS OFFERED THAT JOB ABOARD THE MUSICAL CRUISE SHIP.
SCRUFFLES! QUIT CRYING AND START FIGHTING!
WAK
BAM
HA! YOU MAY HAVE BEATEN ME CREW, BUT YOU'RE STILL NO MATCH FOR ME *MONSTER!* GET THEM, NORBERT! HURT THEM WITH YOUR VIOLENCE!
NORBERT?!
STOP HITTING YOURSELF! STOP HITTING YOURSELF!
QUIT IT! I'M TELLING MOM!

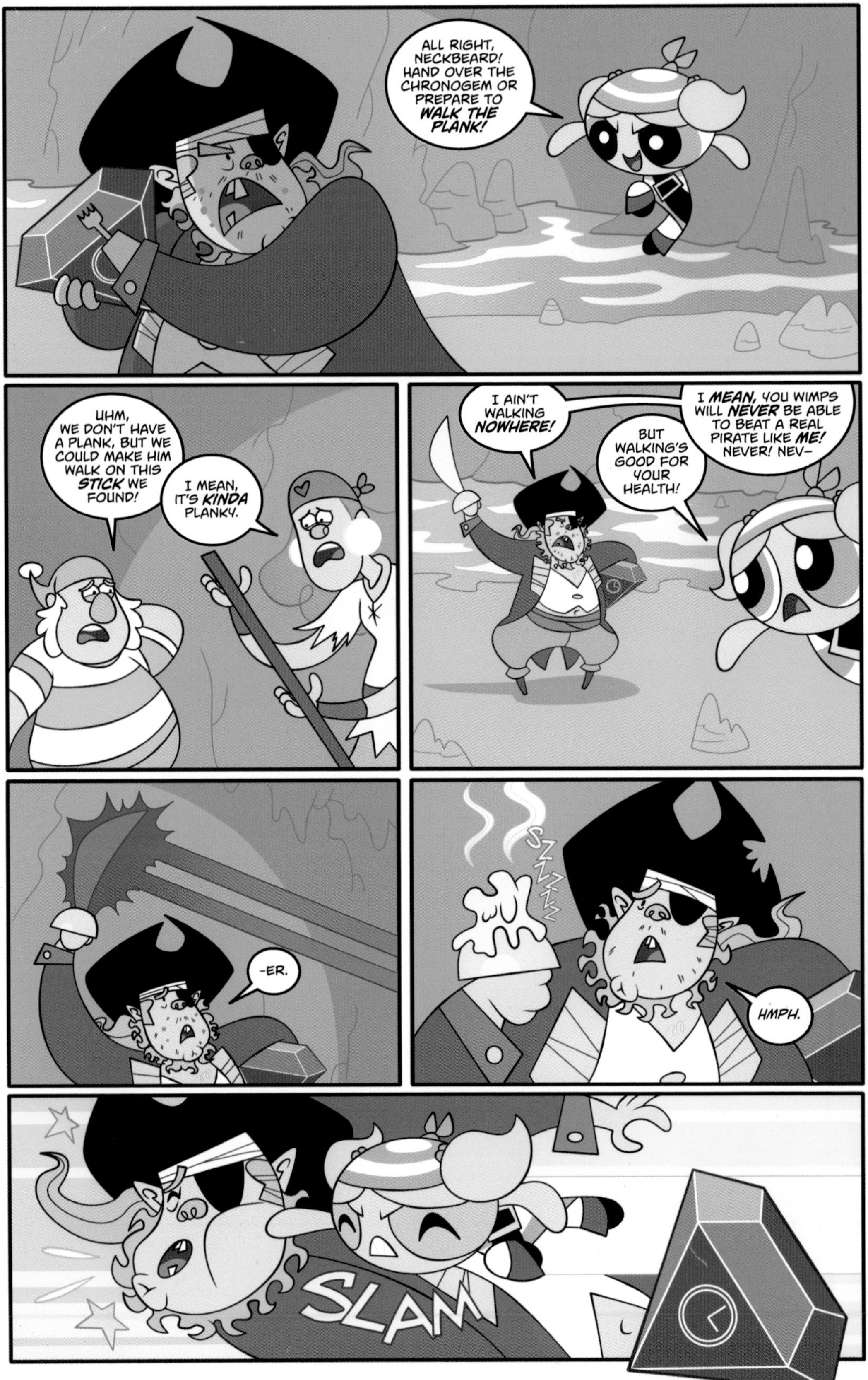
ALL RIGHT, NECKBEARD! HAND OVER THE CHRONOGEM OR PREPARE TO WALK THE PLANK!
UHM, WE DON'T HAVE A PLANK, BUT WE COULD MAKE HIM WALK ON THIS STICK WE FOUND!
I MEAN, IT'S KINDA PLANKY.
I AIN'T WALKING NOWHERE!
BUT WALKING'S GOOD FOR YOUR HEALTH!
I MEAN, YOU WIMPS WILL NEVER BE ABLE TO BEAT A REAL PIRATE LIKE ME! NEVER! NEV–
-ER.
SZZZZZ
HMPH.
SLAM

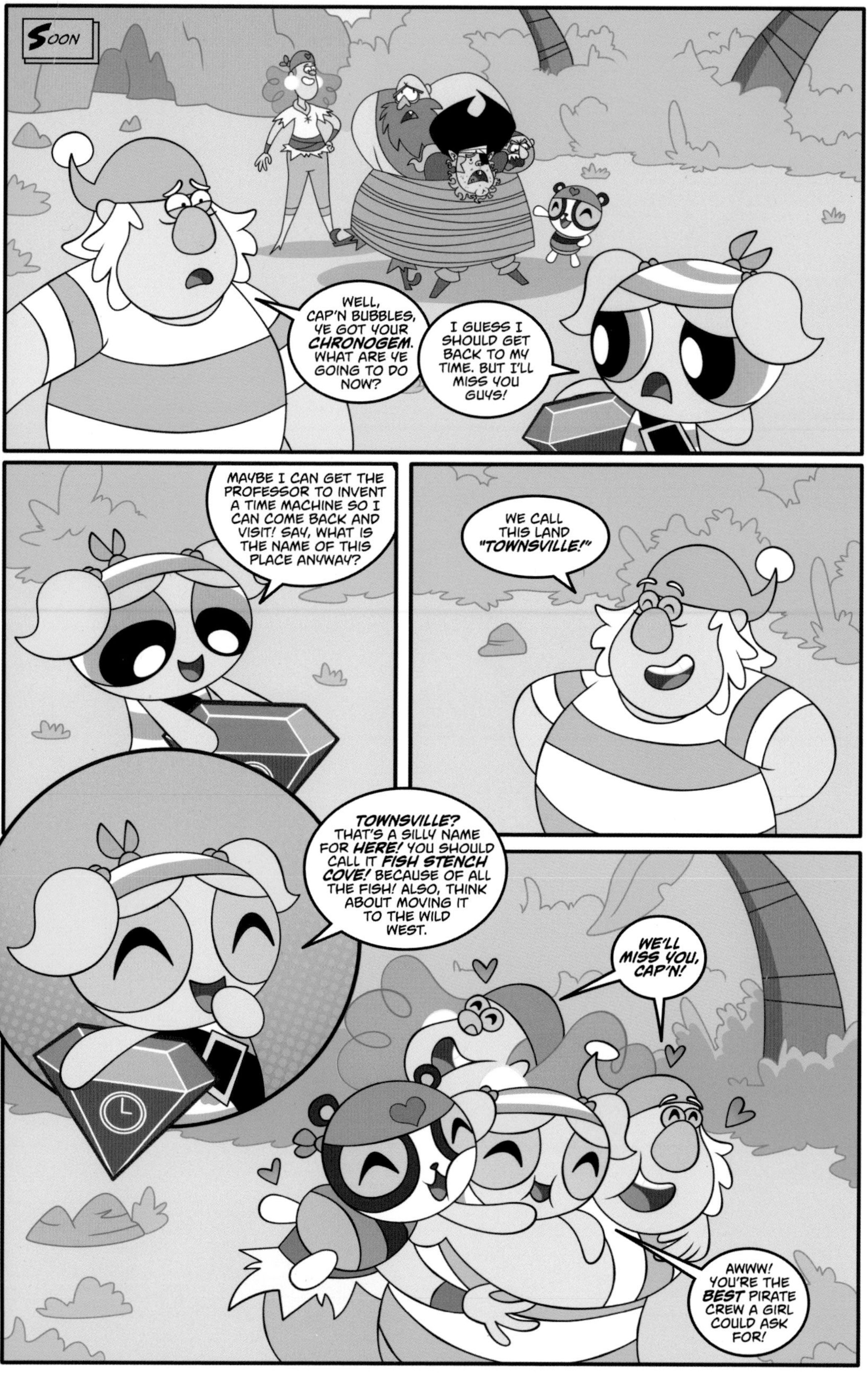
SOON
WELL, CAP'N BUBBLES, YE GOT YOUR CHRONOGEM. WHAT ARE YE GOING TO DO NOW?
I GUESS I SHOULD GET BACK TO MY TIME. BUT I'LL MISS YOU GUYS!
MAYBE I CAN GET THE PROFESSOR TO INVENT A TIME MACHINE SO I CAN COME BACK AND VISIT! SAY, WHAT IS THE NAME OF THIS PLACE ANYWAY?
WE CALL THIS LAND "TOWNSVILLE!"
TOWNSVILLE? THAT'S A SILLY NAME FOR HERE! YOU SHOULD CALL IT FISH STENCH COVE! BECAUSE OF ALL THE FISH! ALSO, THINK ABOUT MOVING IT TO THE WILD WEST.
WE'LL MISS YOU, CAP'N!
AWWW! YOU'RE THE BEST PIRATE CREW A GIRL COULD ASK FOR!

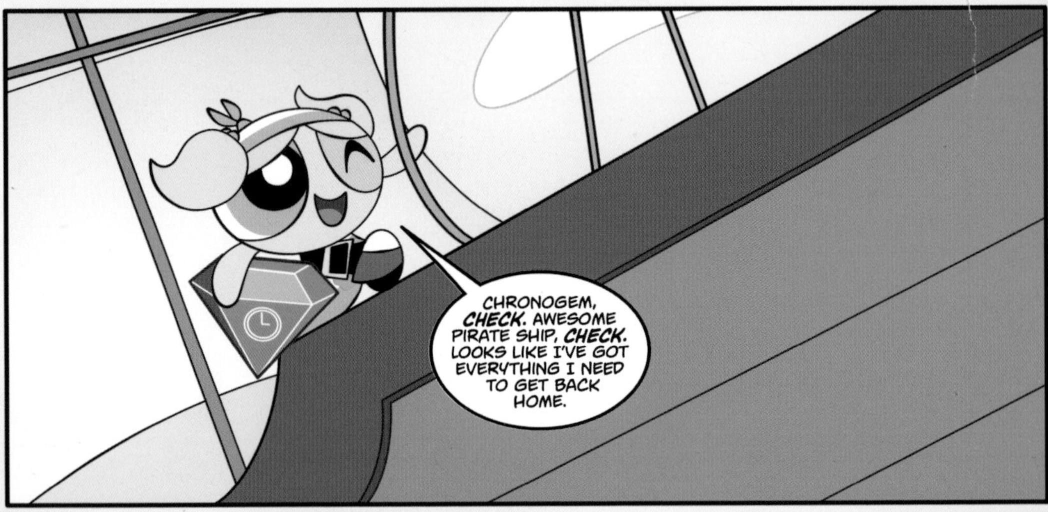
CHRONOGEM, **CHECK.** AWESOME PIRATE SHIP, **CHECK.** LOOKS LIKE I'VE GOT EVERYTHING I NEED TO GET BACK HOME.

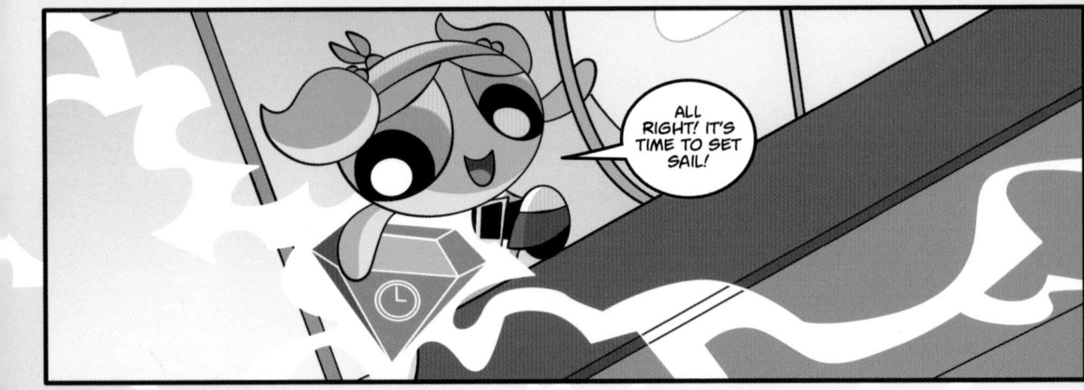
ALL RIGHT! IT'S TIME TO SET SAIL!

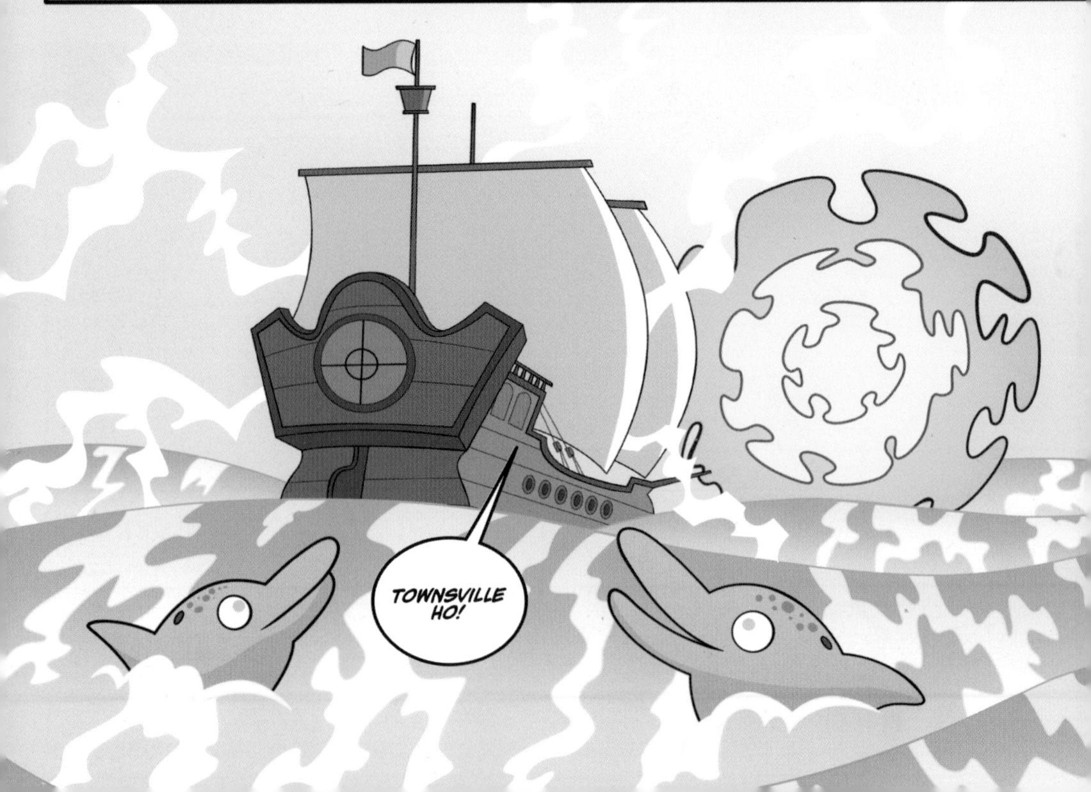
TOWNSVILLE HO!

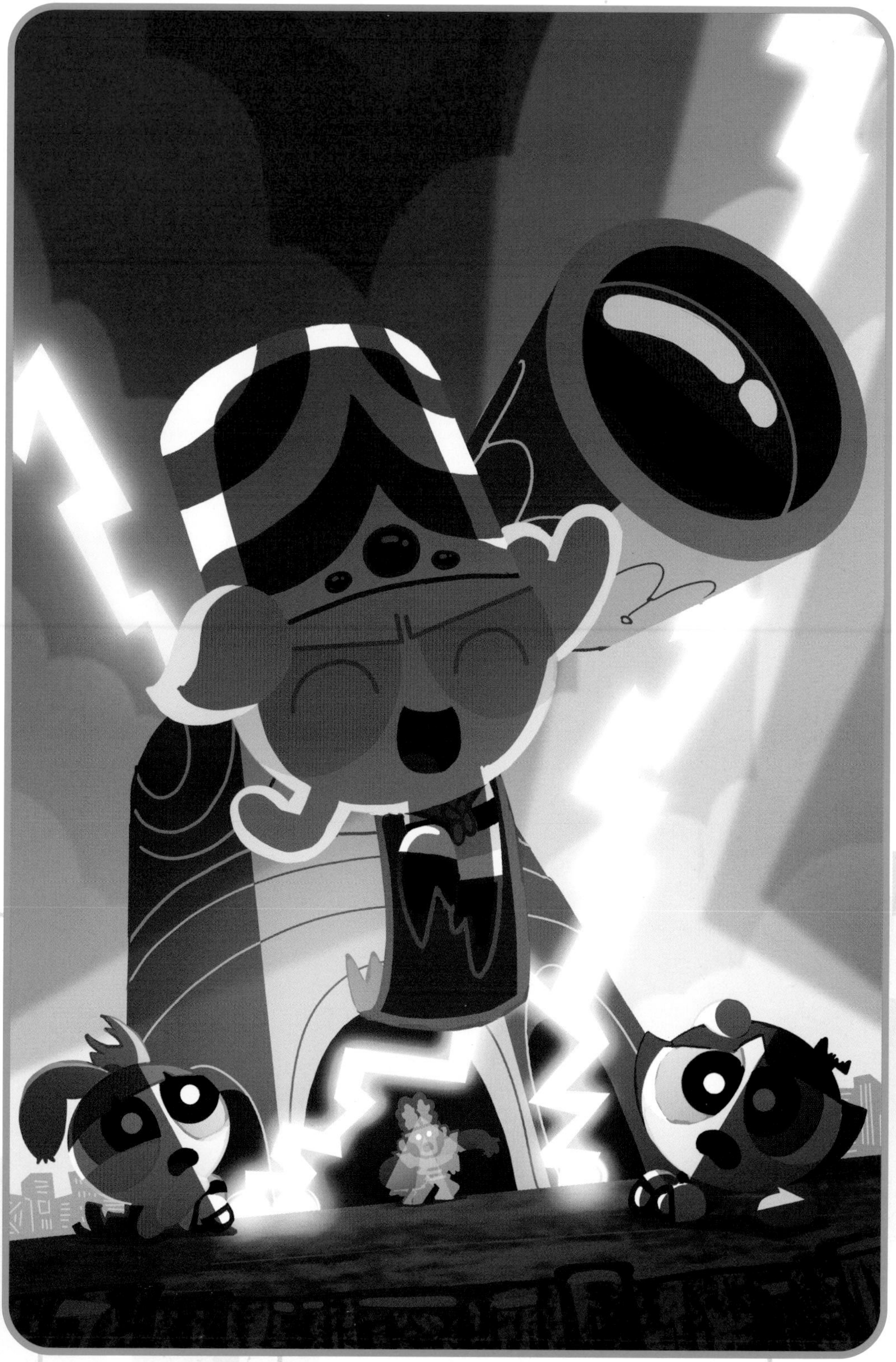

Cover Art by **Kyle Neswald**

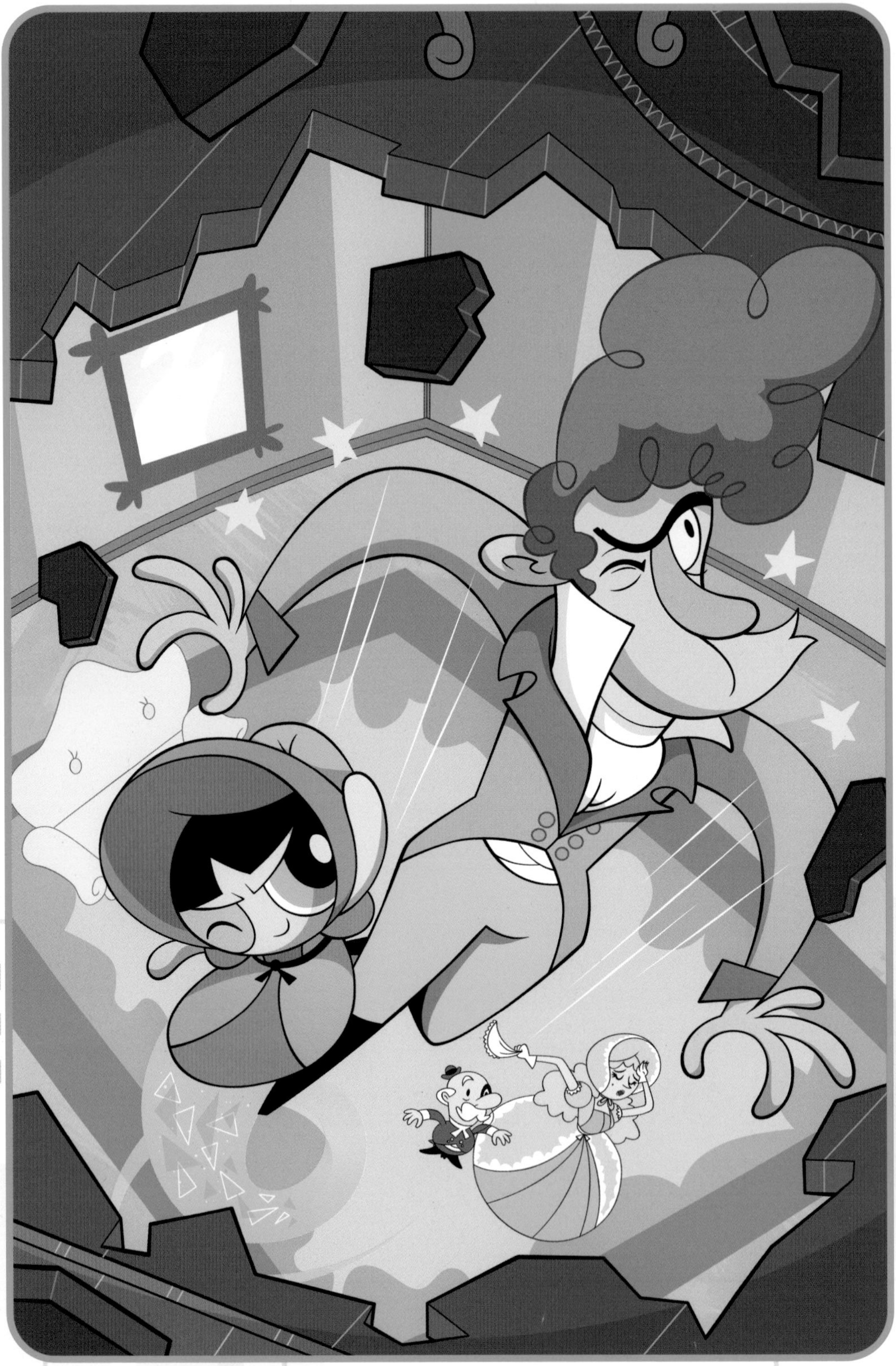

Cover Art by **Philip Murphy**

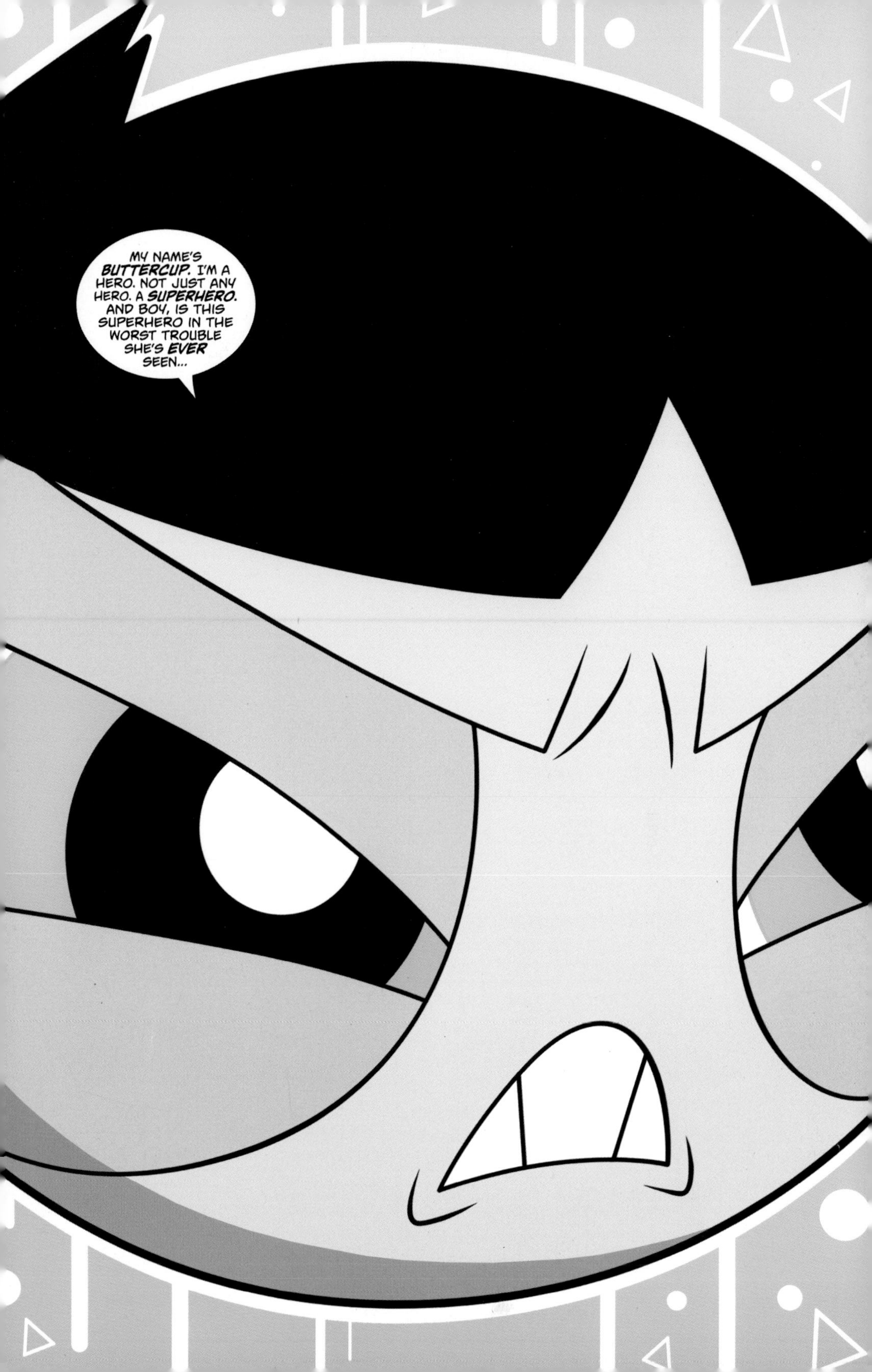
MY NAME'S BUTTERCUP. I'M A HERO. NOT JUST ANY HERO. A SUPERHERO. AND BOY, IS THIS SUPERHERO IN THE WORST TROUBLE SHE'S EVER SEEN...

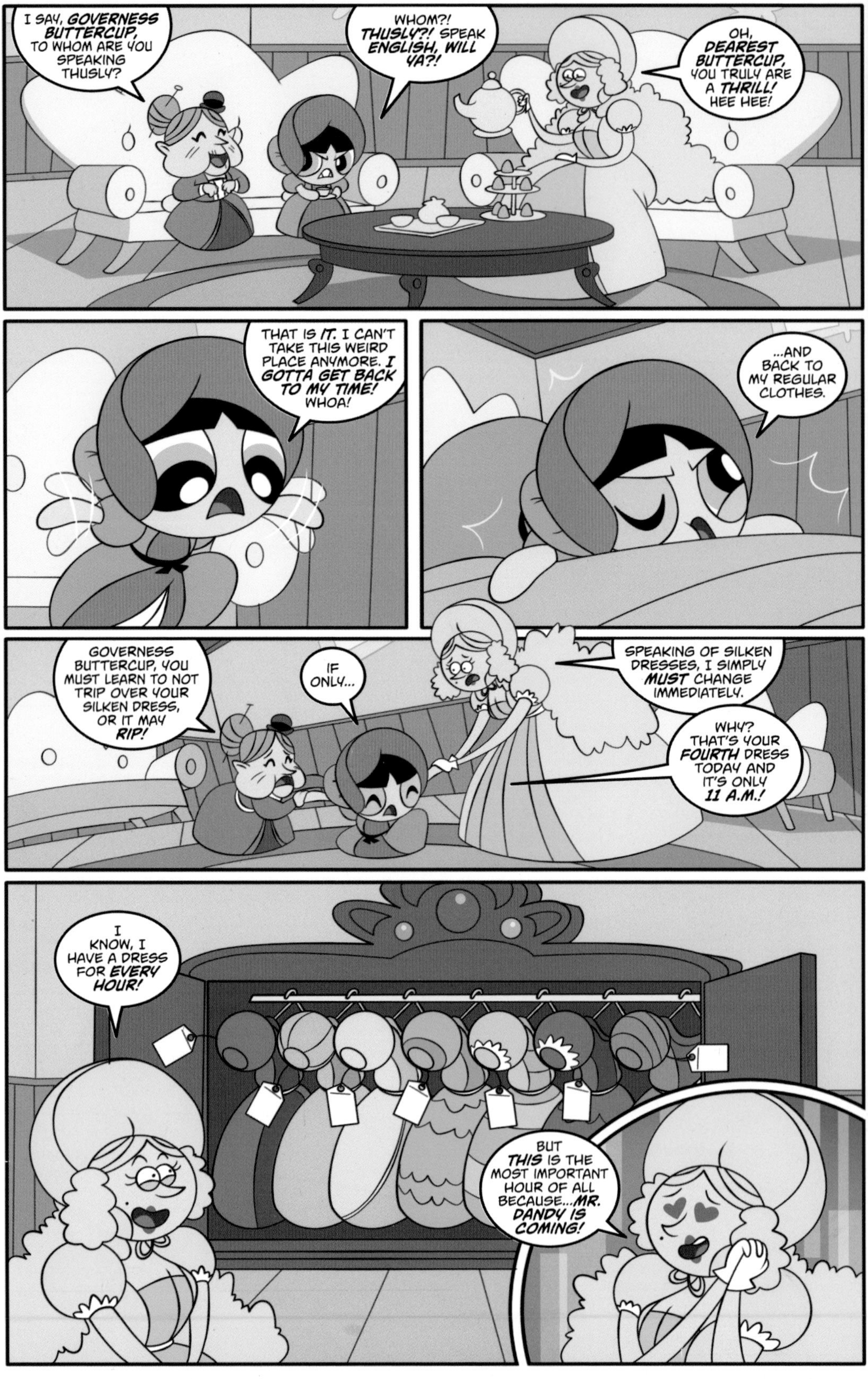
I SAY, GOVERNESS BUTTERCUP, TO WHOM ARE YOU SPEAKING THUSLY?
WHOM?! THUSLY?! SPEAK ENGLISH, WILL YA?!
OH, DEAREST BUTTERCUP, YOU TRULY ARE A THRILL! HEE HEE!
THAT IS IT. I CAN'T TAKE THIS WEIRD PLACE ANYMORE. I GOTTA GET BACK TO MY TIME! WHOA!
...AND BACK TO MY REGULAR CLOTHES.
GOVERNESS BUTTERCUP, YOU MUST LEARN TO NOT TRIP OVER YOUR SILKEN DRESS, OR IT MAY RIP!
IF ONLY...
SPEAKING OF SILKEN DRESSES, I SIMPLY MUST CHANGE IMMEDIATELY.
WHY? THAT'S YOUR FOURTH DRESS TODAY AND IT'S ONLY 11 A.M.!
I KNOW, I HAVE A DRESS FOR EVERY HOUR!
BUT THIS IS THE MOST IMPORTANT HOUR OF ALL BECAUSE...MR. DANDY IS COMING!

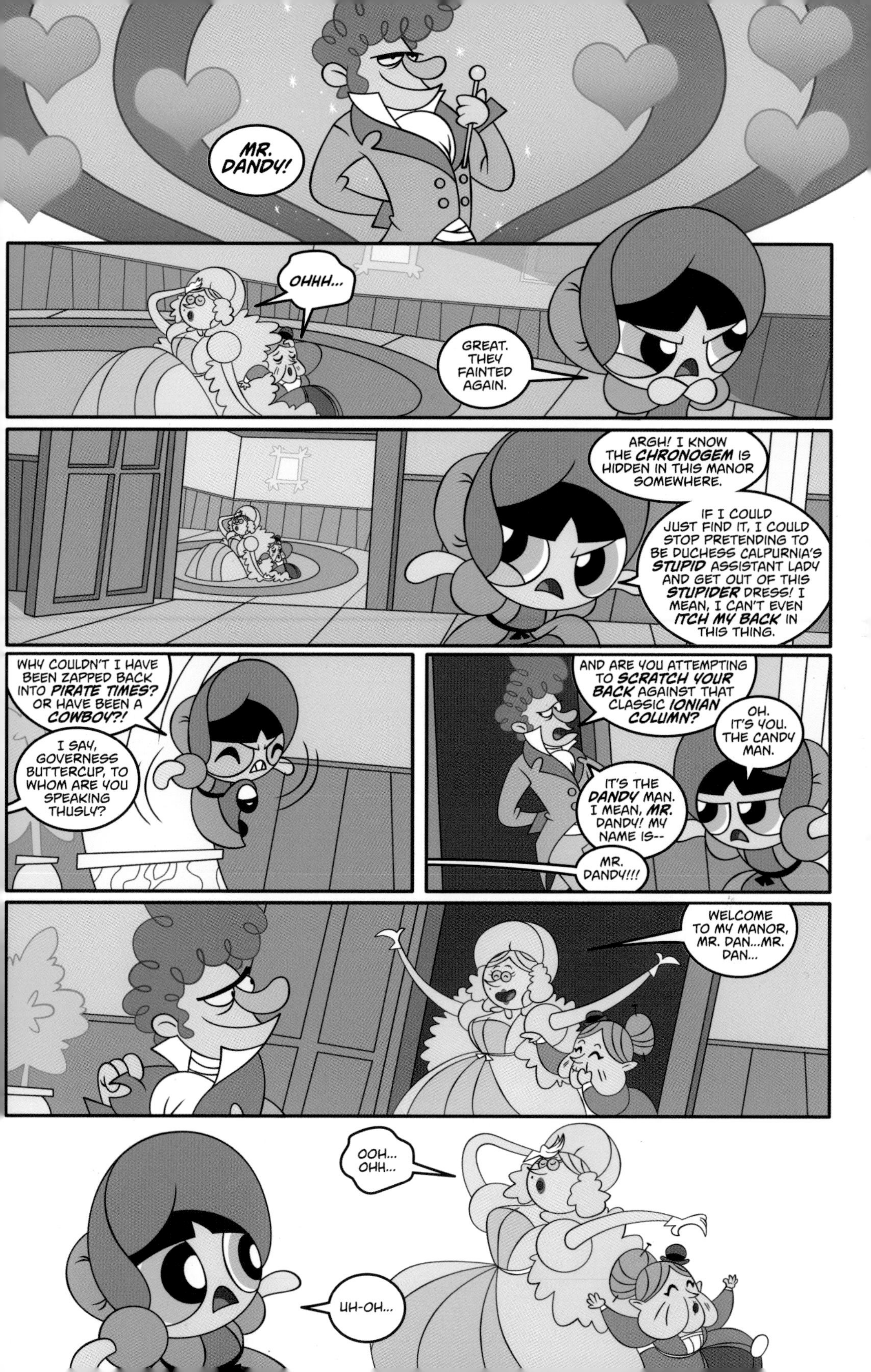
MR. DANDY!
OHHH...
GREAT. THEY FAINTED AGAIN.
ARGH! I KNOW THE CHRONOGEM IS HIDDEN IN THIS MANOR SOMEWHERE.
IF I COULD JUST FIND IT, I COULD STOP PRETENDING TO BE DUCHESS CALPURNIA'S STUPID ASSISTANT LADY AND GET OUT OF THIS STUPIDER DRESS! I MEAN, I CAN'T EVEN ITCH MY BACK IN THIS THING.
WHY COULDN'T I HAVE BEEN ZAPPED BACK INTO PIRATE TIMES? OR HAVE BEEN A COWBOY?!
I SAY, GOVERNESS BUTTERCUP, TO WHOM ARE YOU SPEAKING THUSLY?
AND ARE YOU ATTEMPTING TO SCRATCH YOUR BACK AGAINST THAT CLASSIC IONIAN COLUMN?
OH. IT'S YOU. THE CANDY MAN.
IT'S THE DANDY MAN. I MEAN, MR. DANDY! MY NAME IS--
MR. DANDY!!!
WELCOME TO MY MANOR, MR. DAN...MR. DAN...
OOH... OHH...
UH-OH...

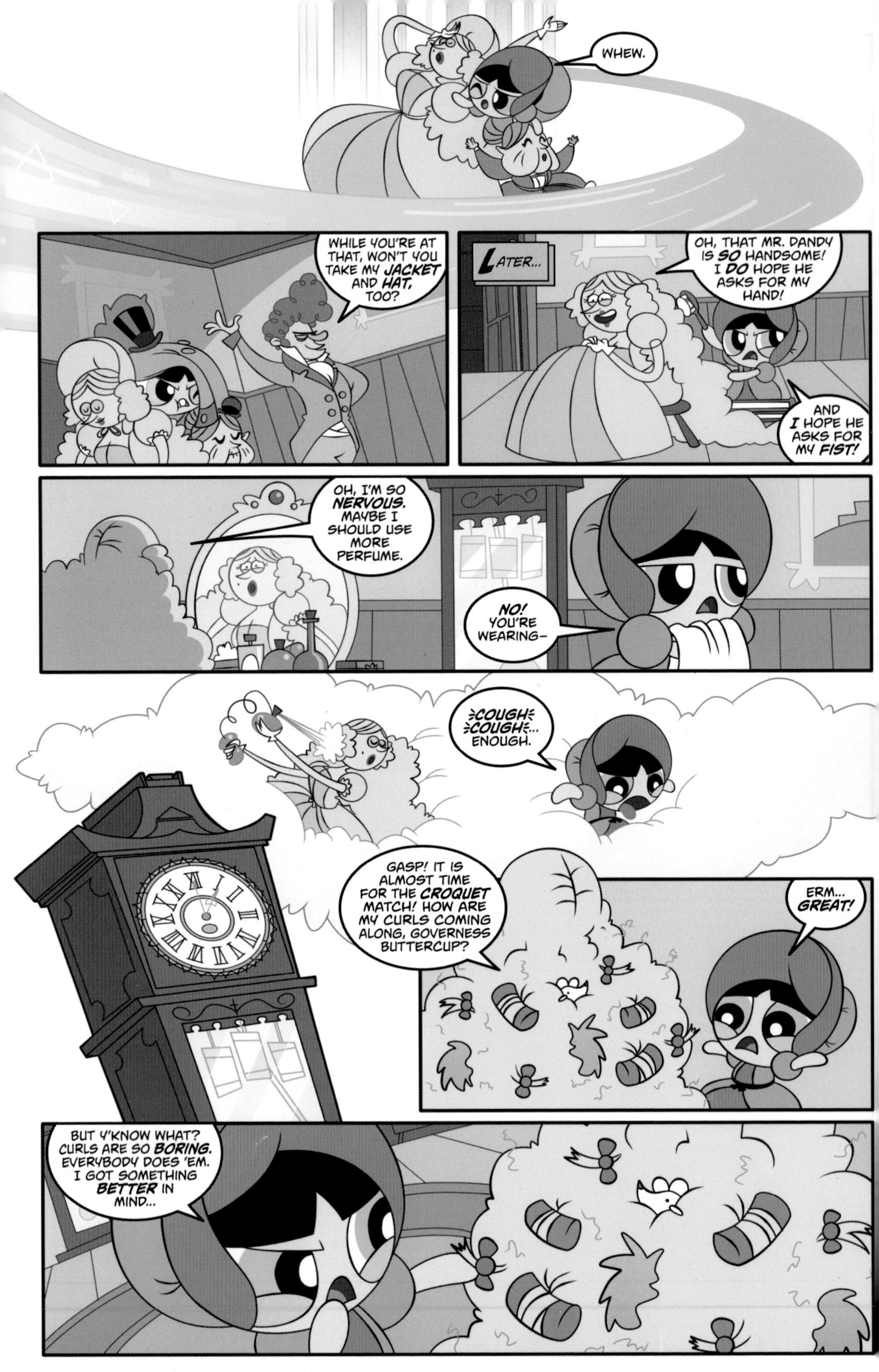
WHEW.
WHILE YOU'RE AT THAT, WON'T YOU TAKE MY JACKET AND HAT, TOO?
LATER...
OH, THAT MR. DANDY IS SO HANDSOME! I DO HOPE HE ASKS FOR MY HAND!
AND I HOPE HE ASKS FOR MY FIST!
OH, I'M SO NERVOUS. MAYBE I SHOULD USE MORE PERFUME.
NO! YOU'RE WEARING—
COUGH COUGH... ENOUGH.
GASP! IT IS ALMOST TIME FOR THE CROQUET MATCH! HOW ARE MY CURLS COMING ALONG, GOVERNESS BUTTERCUP?
ERM... GREAT!
BUT Y'KNOW WHAT? CURLS ARE SO BORING. EVERYBODY DOES 'EM. I GOT SOMETHING BETTER IN MIND...

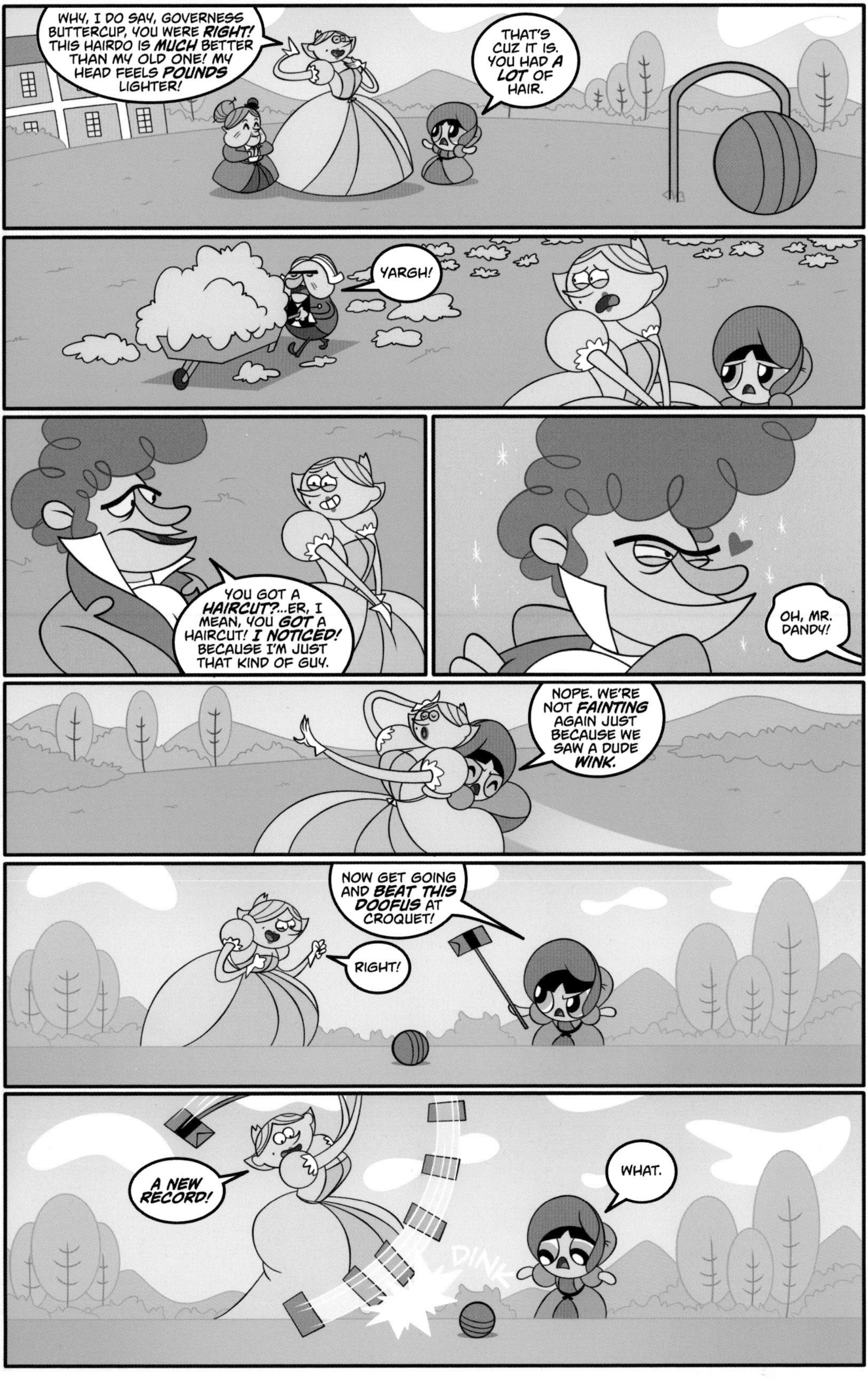
WHY, I DO SAY, GOVERNESS BUTTERCUP, YOU WERE RIGHT! THIS HAIRDO IS MUCH BETTER THAN MY OLD ONE! MY HEAD FEELS POUNDS LIGHTER!
THAT'S CUZ IT IS. YOU HAD A LOT OF HAIR.
YARGH!
YOU GOT A HAIRCUT?...ER, I MEAN, YOU GOT A HAIRCUT! I NOTICED! BECAUSE I'M JUST THAT KIND OF GUY.
OH, MR. DANDY!
NOPE. WE'RE NOT FAINTING AGAIN JUST BECAUSE WE SAW A DUDE WINK.
NOW GET GOING AND BEAT THIS DOOFUS AT CROQUET!
RIGHT!
A NEW RECORD!
WHAT.
DINK

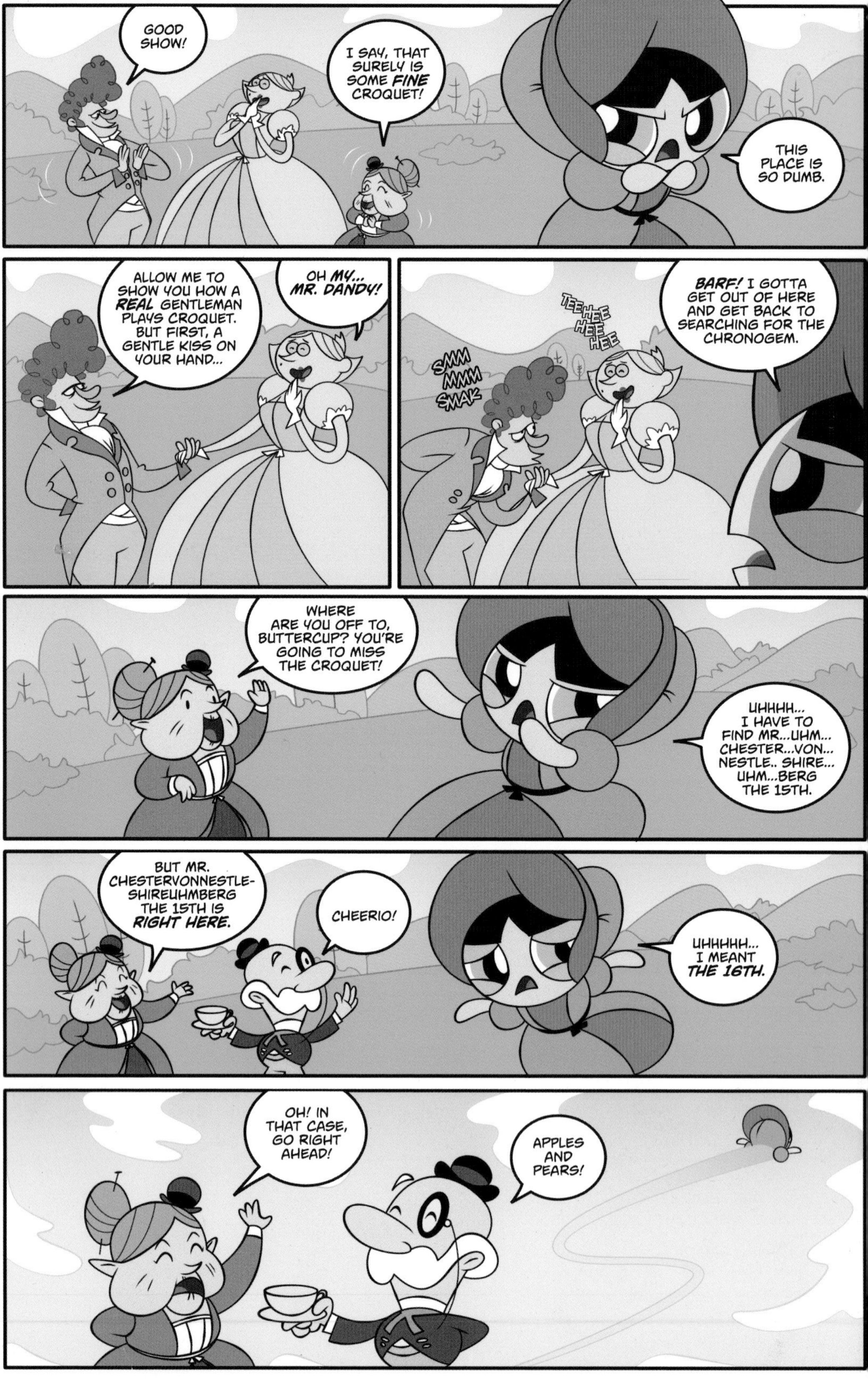
GOOD SHOW!
I SAY, THAT SURELY IS SOME FINE CROQUET!
THIS PLACE IS SO DUMB.
ALLOW ME TO SHOW YOU HOW A REAL GENTLEMAN PLAYS CROQUET. BUT FIRST, A GENTLE KISS ON YOUR HAND...
OH MY... MR. DANDY!
SMM MMM SMAK
TEEHEE HEE HEE
BARF! I GOTTA GET OUT OF HERE AND GET BACK TO SEARCHING FOR THE CHRONOGEM.
WHERE ARE YOU OFF TO, BUTTERCUP? YOU'RE GOING TO MISS THE CROQUET!
UHHHH... I HAVE TO FIND MR...UHM... CHESTER...VON... NESTLE.. SHIRE... UHM...BERG THE 15TH.
BUT MR. CHESTERVONNESTLE-SHIREUHMBERG THE 15TH IS RIGHT HERE.
CHEERIO!
UHHHHH... I MEANT THE 16TH.
OH! IN THAT CASE, GO RIGHT AHEAD!
APPLES AND PEARS!

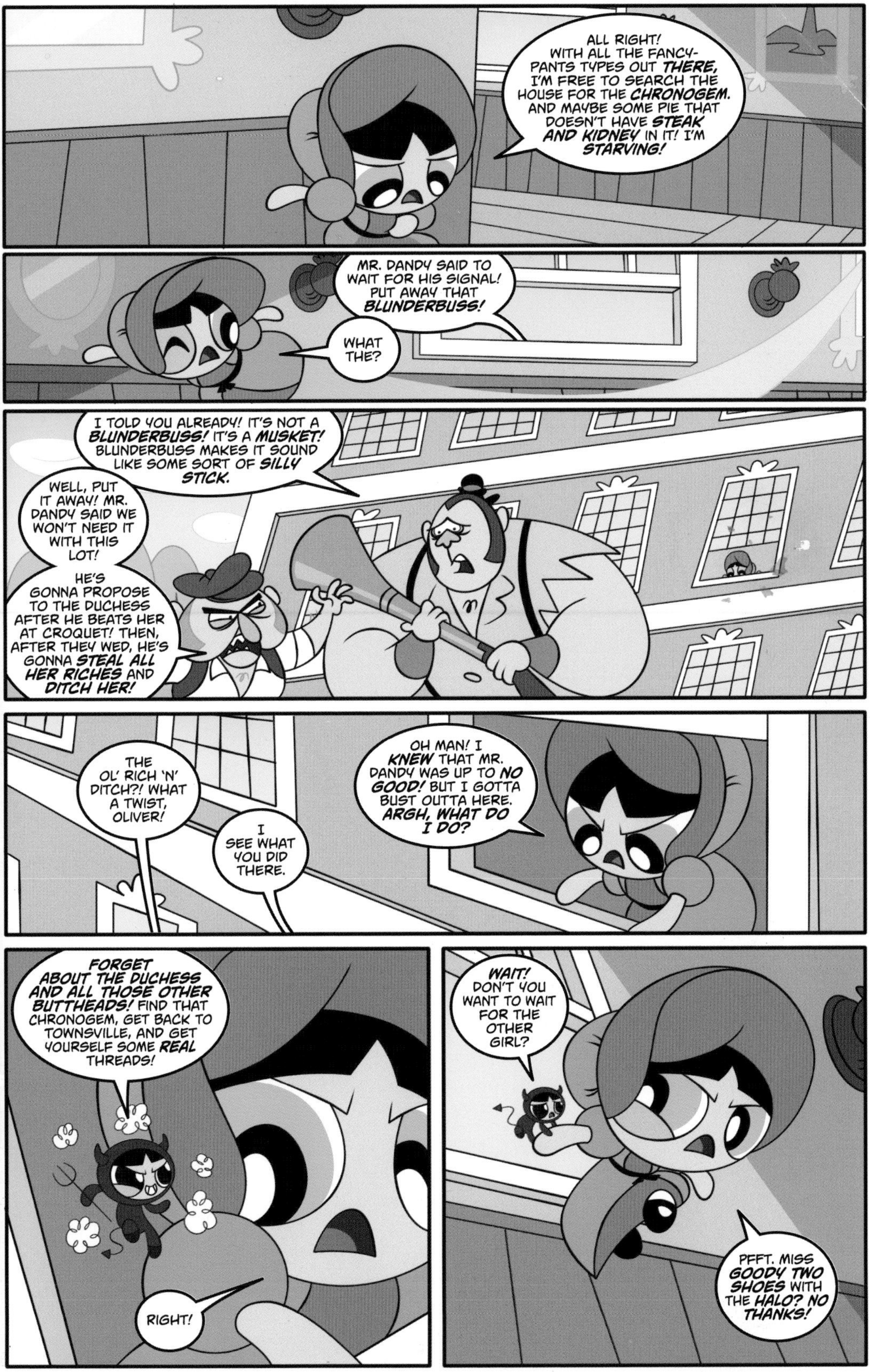
ALL RIGHT! WITH ALL THE FANCY-PANTS TYPES OUT THERE, I'M FREE TO SEARCH THE HOUSE FOR THE CHRONOGEM. AND MAYBE SOME PIE THAT DOESN'T HAVE STEAK AND KIDNEY IN IT! I'M STARVING!
MR. DANDY SAID TO WAIT FOR HIS SIGNAL! PUT AWAY THAT BLUNDERBUSS!
WHAT THE?
I TOLD YOU ALREADY! IT'S NOT A BLUNDERBUSS! IT'S A MUSKET! BLUNDERBUSS MAKES IT SOUND LIKE SOME SORT OF SILLY STICK.
WELL, PUT IT AWAY! MR. DANDY SAID WE WON'T NEED IT WITH THIS LOT!
HE'S GONNA PROPOSE TO THE DUCHESS AFTER HE BEATS HER AT CROQUET! THEN, AFTER THEY WED, HE'S GONNA STEAL ALL HER RICHES AND DITCH HER!
THE OL' RICH 'N' DITCH?! WHAT A TWIST, OLIVER!
I SEE WHAT YOU DID THERE.
OH MAN! I KNEW THAT MR. DANDY WAS UP TO NO GOOD! BUT I GOTTA BUST OUTTA HERE. ARGH, WHAT DO I DO?
FORGET ABOUT THE DUCHESS AND ALL THOSE OTHER BUTTHEADS! FIND THAT CHRONOGEM, GET BACK TO TOWNSVILLE, AND GET YOURSELF SOME REAL THREADS!
RIGHT!
WAIT! DON'T YOU WANT TO WAIT FOR THE OTHER GIRL?
PFFT. MISS GOODY TWO SHOES WITH THE HALO? NO THANKS!

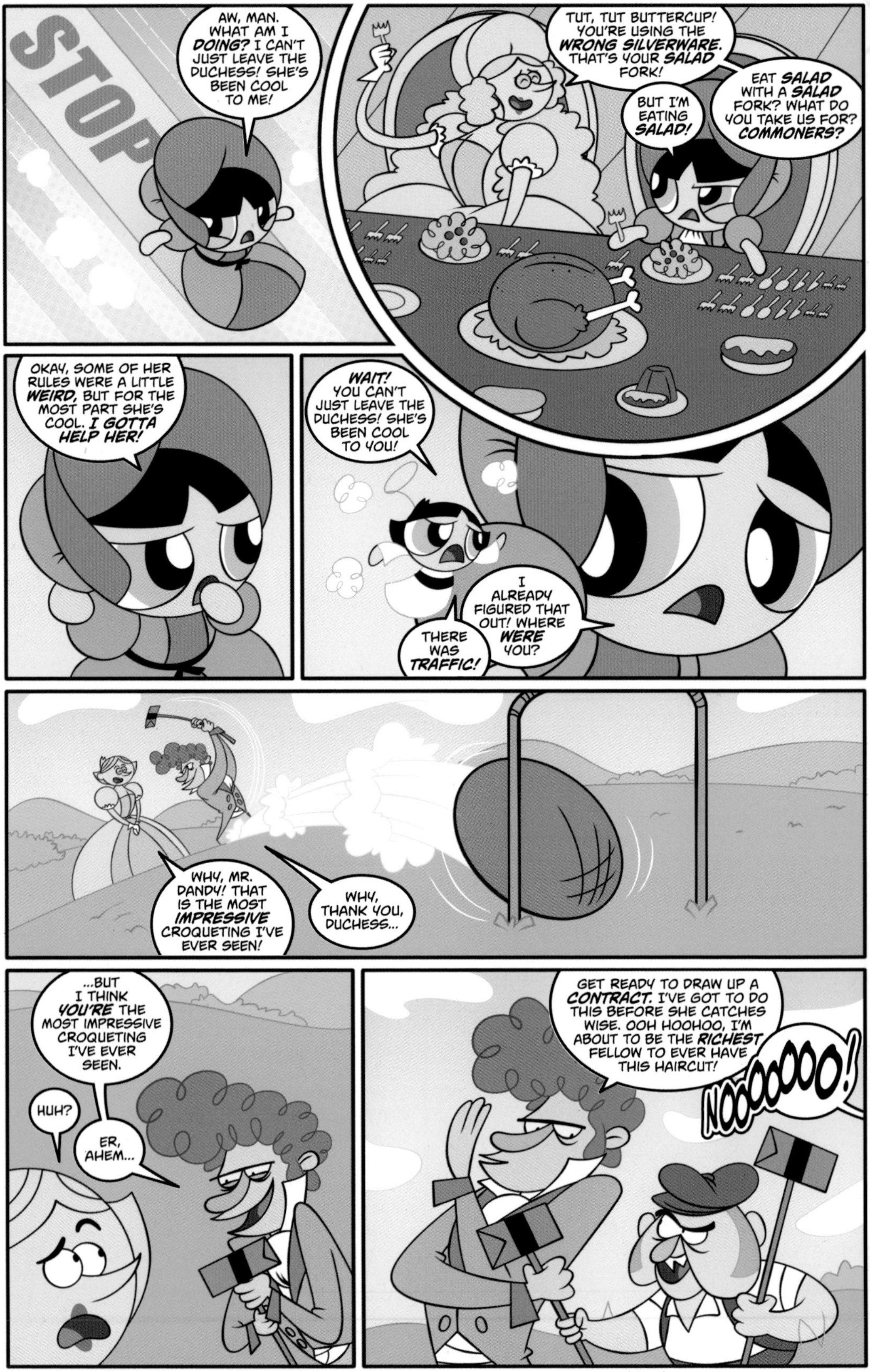
STOP
AW, MAN. WHAT AM I DOING? I CAN'T JUST LEAVE THE DUCHESS! SHE'S BEEN COOL TO ME!
TUT, TUT BUTTERCUP! YOU'RE USING THE WRONG SILVERWARE. THAT'S YOUR SALAD FORK!
BUT I'M EATING SALAD!
EAT SALAD WITH A SALAD FORK? WHAT DO YOU TAKE US FOR? COMMONERS?
OKAY, SOME OF HER RULES WERE A LITTLE WEIRD, BUT FOR THE MOST PART SHE'S COOL. I GOTTA HELP HER!
WAIT! YOU CAN'T JUST LEAVE THE DUCHESS! SHE'S BEEN COOL TO YOU!
I ALREADY FIGURED THAT OUT! WHERE WERE YOU?
THERE WAS TRAFFIC!
WHY, MR. DANDY! THAT IS THE MOST IMPRESSIVE CROQUETING I'VE EVER SEEN!
WHY, THANK YOU, DUCHESS...
...BUT I THINK YOU'RE THE MOST IMPRESSIVE CROQUETING I'VE EVER SEEN.
HUH?
ER, AHEM...
GET READY TO DRAW UP A CONTRACT. I'VE GOT TO DO THIS BEFORE SHE CATCHES WISE. OOH HOOHOO, I'M ABOUT TO BE THE RICHEST FELLOW TO EVER HAVE THIS HAIRCUT!
NOOOOOOO!

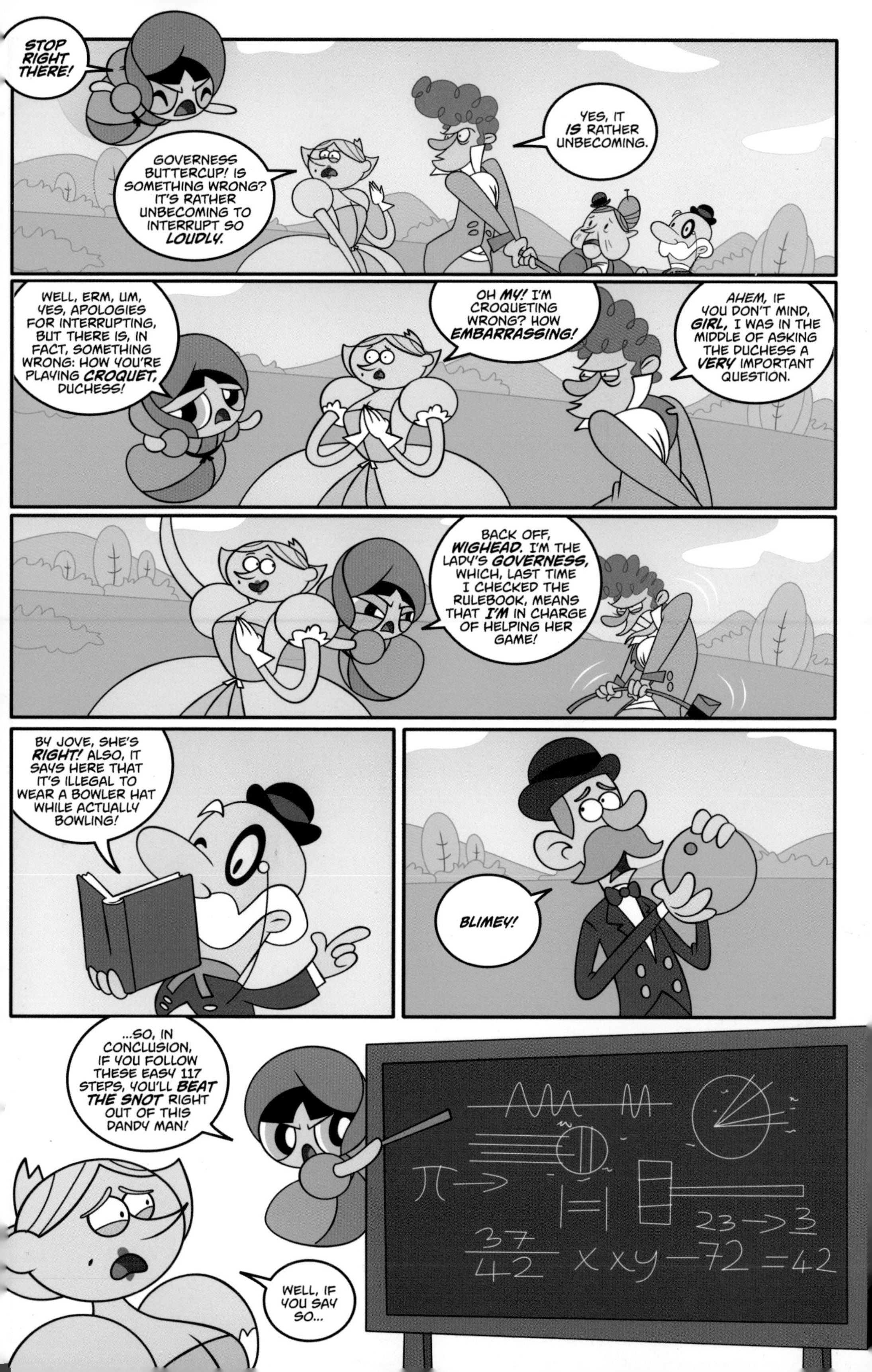
STOP RIGHT THERE!
GOVERNESS BUTTERCUP! IS SOMETHING WRONG? IT'S RATHER UNBECOMING TO INTERRUPT SO LOUDLY.
YES, IT IS RATHER UNBECOMING.
WELL, ERM, UM, YES, APOLOGIES FOR INTERRUPTING, BUT THERE IS, IN FACT, SOMETHING WRONG: HOW YOU'RE PLAYING CROQUET, DUCHESS!
OH MY! I'M CROQUETING WRONG? HOW EMBARRASSING!
AHEM, IF YOU DON'T MIND, GIRL, I WAS IN THE MIDDLE OF ASKING THE DUCHESS A VERY IMPORTANT QUESTION.
BACK OFF, WIGHEAD. I'M THE LADY'S GOVERNESS, WHICH, LAST TIME I CHECKED THE RULEBOOK, MEANS THAT I'M IN CHARGE OF HELPING HER GAME!
BY JOVE, SHE'S RIGHT! ALSO, IT SAYS HERE THAT IT'S ILLEGAL TO WEAR A BOWLER HAT WHILE ACTUALLY BOWLING!
BLIMEY!
...SO, IN CONCLUSION, IF YOU FOLLOW THESE EASY 117 STEPS, YOU'LL BEAT THE SNOT RIGHT OUT OF THIS DANDY MAN!
WELL, IF YOU SAY SO...

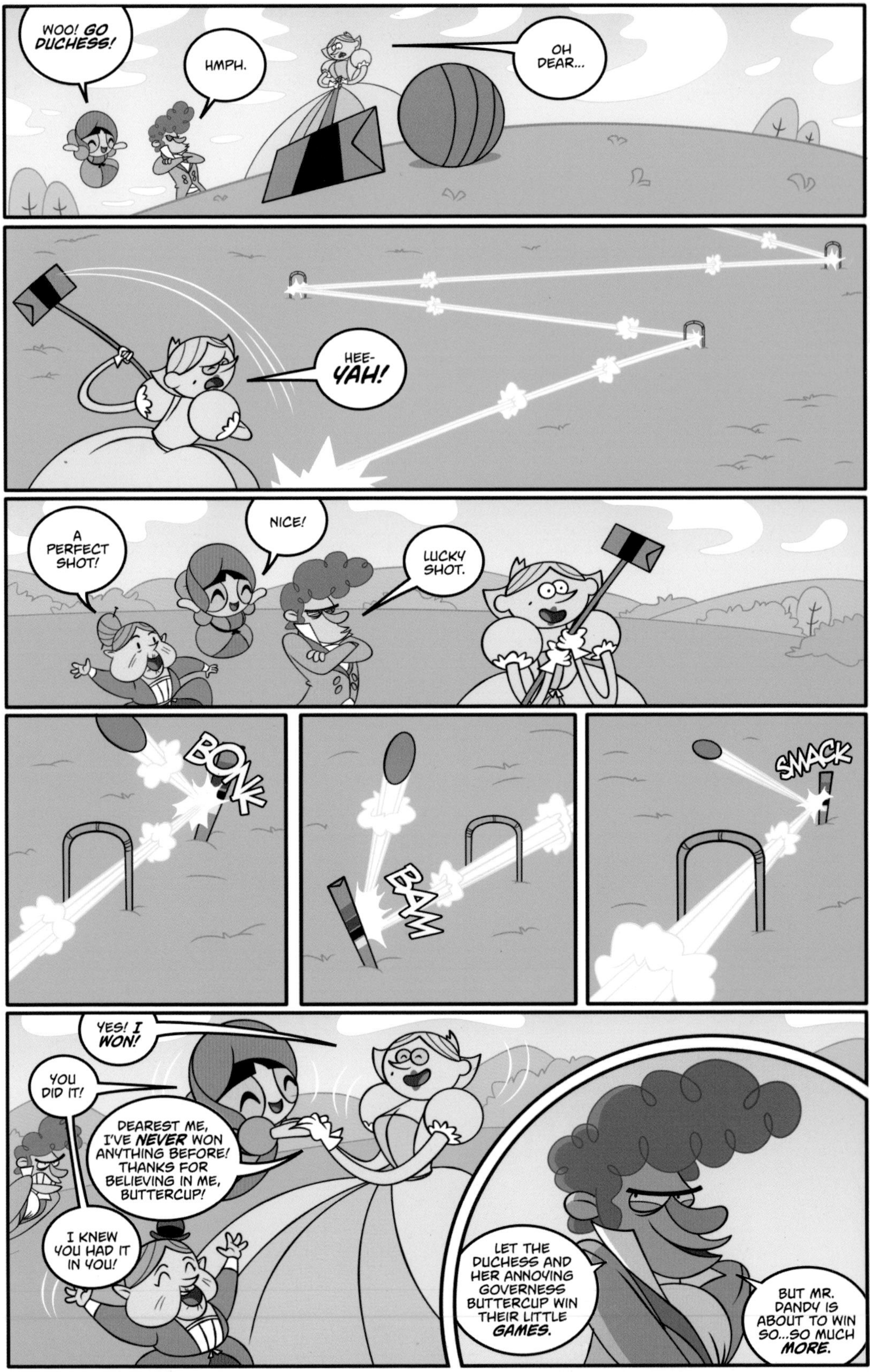
WOO! GO DUCHESS!
HMPH.
OH DEAR...
HEE-YAH!
A PERFECT SHOT!
NICE!
LUCKY SHOT.
BONK
BAM
SMACK
YES! I WON!
YOU DID IT!
DEAREST ME, I'VE NEVER WON ANYTHING BEFORE! THANKS FOR BELIEVING IN ME, BUTTERCUP!
I KNEW YOU HAD IT IN YOU!
LET THE DUCHESS AND HER ANNOYING GOVERNESS BUTTERCUP WIN THEIR LITTLE GAMES.
BUT MR. DANDY IS ABOUT TO WIN SO...SO MUCH MORE.

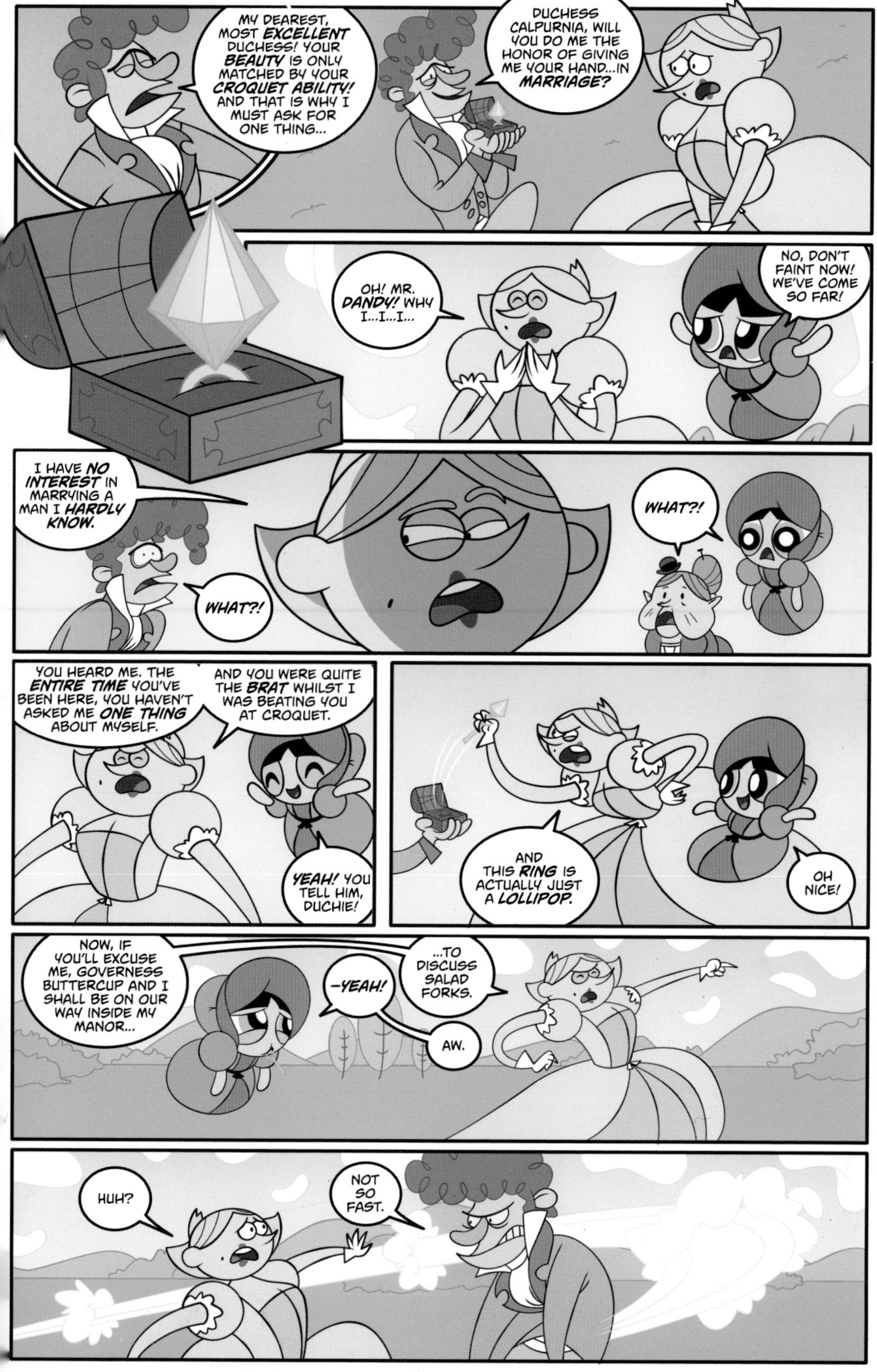
MY DEAREST, MOST EXCELLENT DUCHESS! YOUR BEAUTY IS ONLY MATCHED BY YOUR CROQUET ABILITY! AND THAT IS WHY I MUST ASK FOR ONE THING...
DUCHESS CALPURNIA, WILL YOU DO ME THE HONOR OF GIVING ME YOUR HAND...IN MARRIAGE?
OH! MR. DANDY! WHY I...I...I...
NO, DON'T FAINT NOW! WE'VE COME SO FAR!
I HAVE NO INTEREST IN MARRYING A MAN I HARDLY KNOW.
WHAT?!
WHAT?!
YOU HEARD ME. THE ENTIRE TIME YOU'VE BEEN HERE, YOU HAVEN'T ASKED ME ONE THING ABOUT MYSELF.
AND YOU WERE QUITE THE BRAT WHILST I WAS BEATING YOU AT CROQUET.
YEAH! YOU TELL HIM, DUCHIE!
AND THIS RING IS ACTUALLY JUST A LOLLIPOP.
OH NICE!
NOW, IF YOU'LL EXCUSE ME, GOVERNESS BUTTERCUP AND I SHALL BE ON OUR WAY INSIDE MY MANOR...
–YEAH!
...TO DISCUSS SALAD FORKS.
AW.
HUH?
NOT SO FAST.

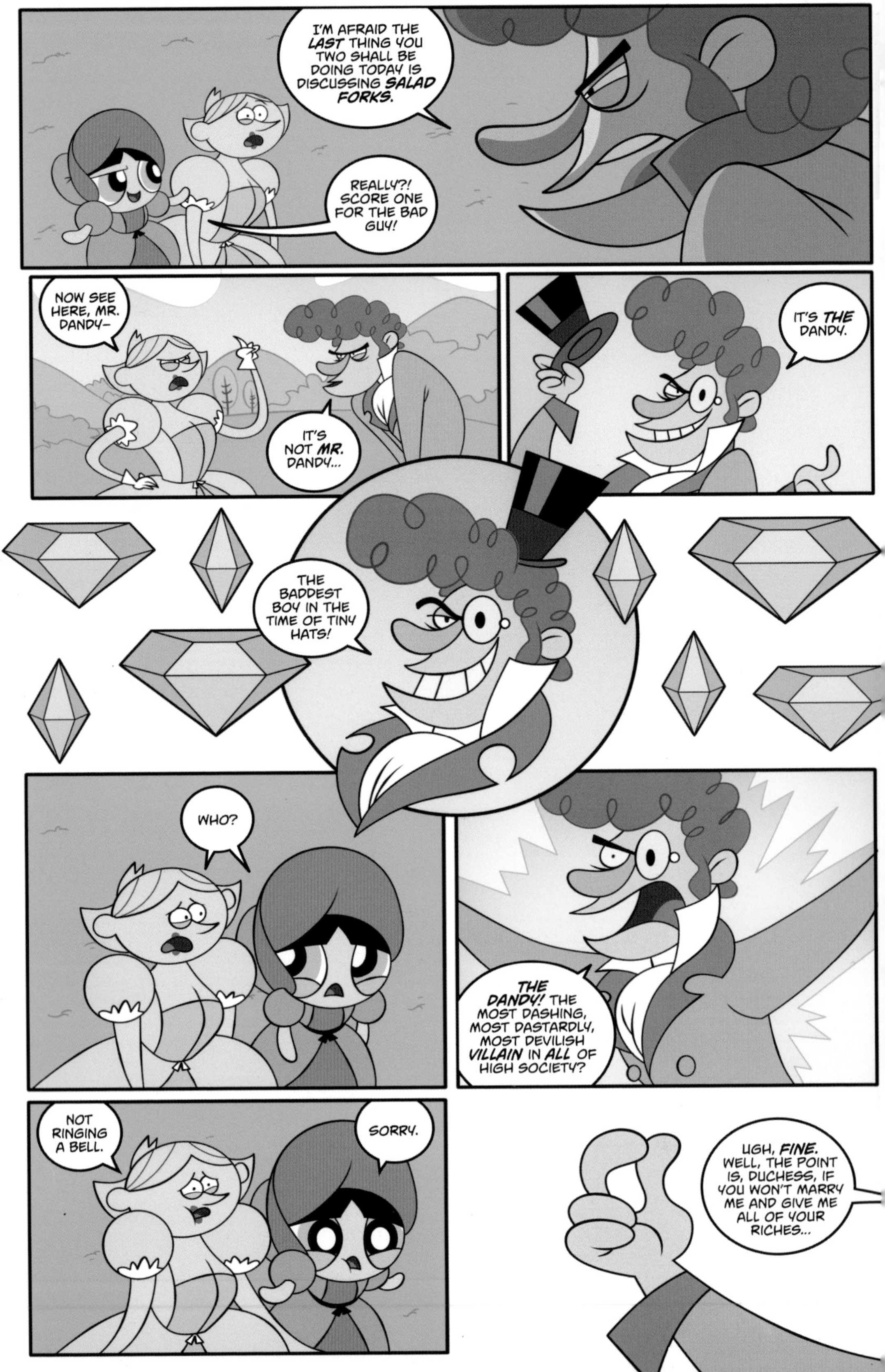
I'M AFRAID THE LAST THING YOU TWO SHALL BE DOING TODAY IS DISCUSSING SALAD FORKS.
REALLY?! SCORE ONE FOR THE BAD GUY!
NOW SEE HERE, MR. DANDY–
IT'S NOT MR. DANDY...
IT'S THE DANDY.
THE BADDEST BOY IN THE TIME OF TINY HATS!
WHO?
THE DANDY! THE MOST DASHING, MOST DASTARDLY, MOST DEVILISH VILLAIN IN ALL OF HIGH SOCIETY?
NOT RINGING A BELL.
SORRY.
UGH, FINE. WELL, THE POINT IS, DUCHESS, IF YOU WON'T MARRY ME AND GIVE ME ALL OF YOUR RICHES...

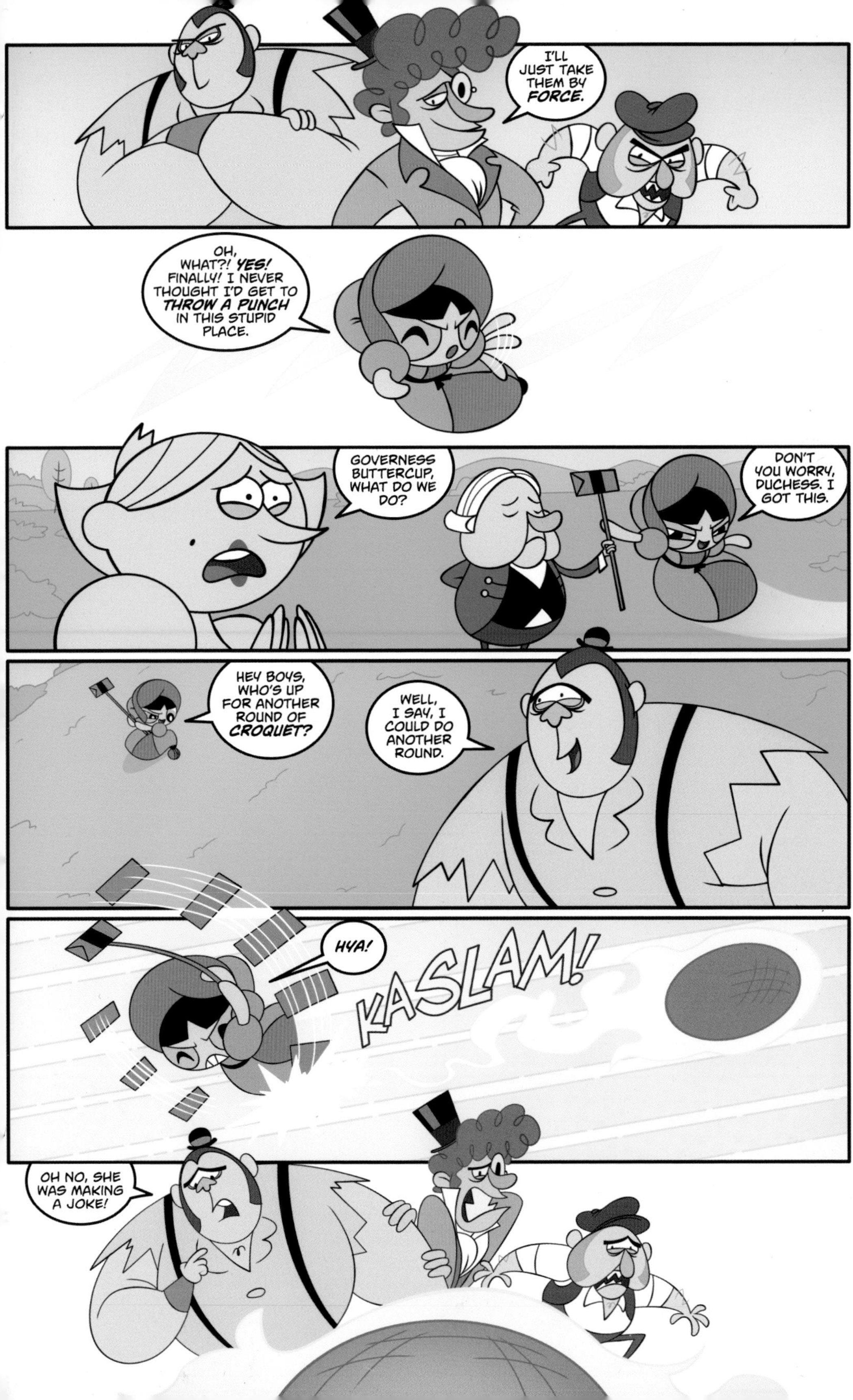
I'LL JUST TAKE THEM BY FORCE.
OH, WHAT?! YES! FINALLY! I NEVER THOUGHT I'D GET TO THROW A PUNCH IN THIS STUPID PLACE.
GOVERNESS BUTTERCUP, WHAT DO WE DO?
DON'T YOU WORRY, DUCHESS. I GOT THIS.
HEY BOYS, WHO'S UP FOR ANOTHER ROUND OF CROQUET?
WELL, I SAY, I COULD DO ANOTHER ROUND.
HYA!
KASLAM!
OH NO, SHE WAS MAKING A JOKE!

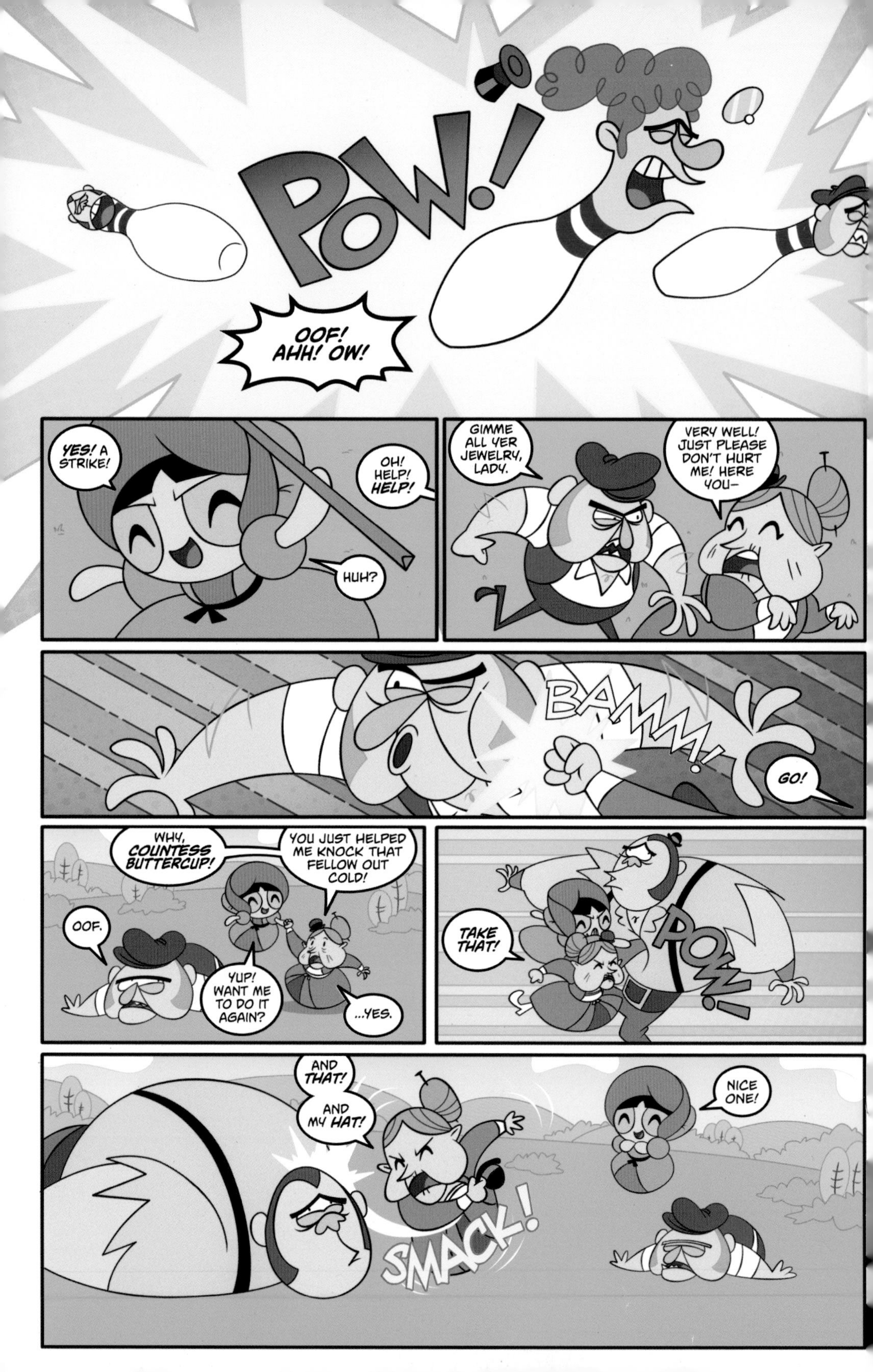
POW!
OOF! AHH! OW!
YES! A STRIKE!
OH! HELP! HELP!
HUH?
GIMME ALL YER JEWELRY, LADY.
VERY WELL! JUST PLEASE DON'T HURT ME! HERE YOU—
BAMMM!
GO!
WHY, COUNTESS BUTTERCUP!
YOU JUST HELPED ME KNOCK THAT FELLOW OUT COLD!
OOF.
YUP! WANT ME TO DO IT AGAIN?
...YES.
TAKE THAT!
POW!
AND THAT!
AND MY HAT!
NICE ONE!
SMACK!

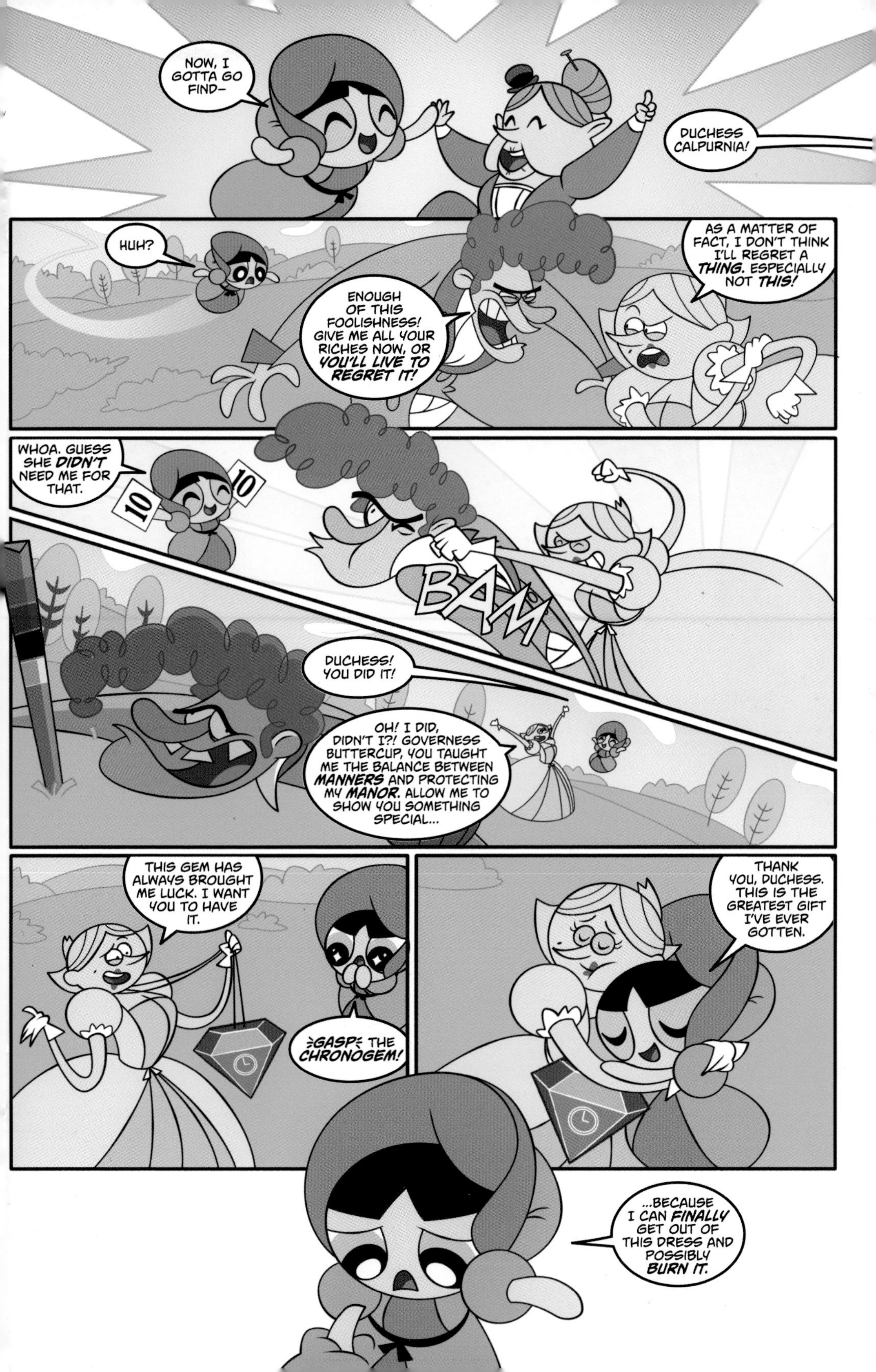
NOW, I GOTTA GO FIND–
DUCHESS CALPURNIA!
HUH?
ENOUGH OF THIS FOOLISHNESS! GIVE ME ALL YOUR RICHES NOW, OR YOU'LL LIVE TO REGRET IT!
AS A MATTER OF FACT, I DON'T THINK I'LL REGRET A THING. ESPECIALLY NOT THIS!
WHOA. GUESS SHE DIDN'T NEED ME FOR THAT.
10
10
BAM
DUCHESS! YOU DID IT!
OH! I DID, DIDN'T I?! GOVERNESS BUTTERCUP, YOU TAUGHT ME THE BALANCE BETWEEN MANNERS AND PROTECTING MY MANOR. ALLOW ME TO SHOW YOU SOMETHING SPECIAL...
THIS GEM HAS ALWAYS BROUGHT ME LUCK. I WANT YOU TO HAVE IT.
GASP THE CHRONOGEM!
THANK YOU, DUCHESS. THIS IS THE GREATEST GIFT I'VE EVER GOTTEN.
...BECAUSE I CAN FINALLY GET OUT OF THIS DRESS AND POSSIBLY BURN IT.

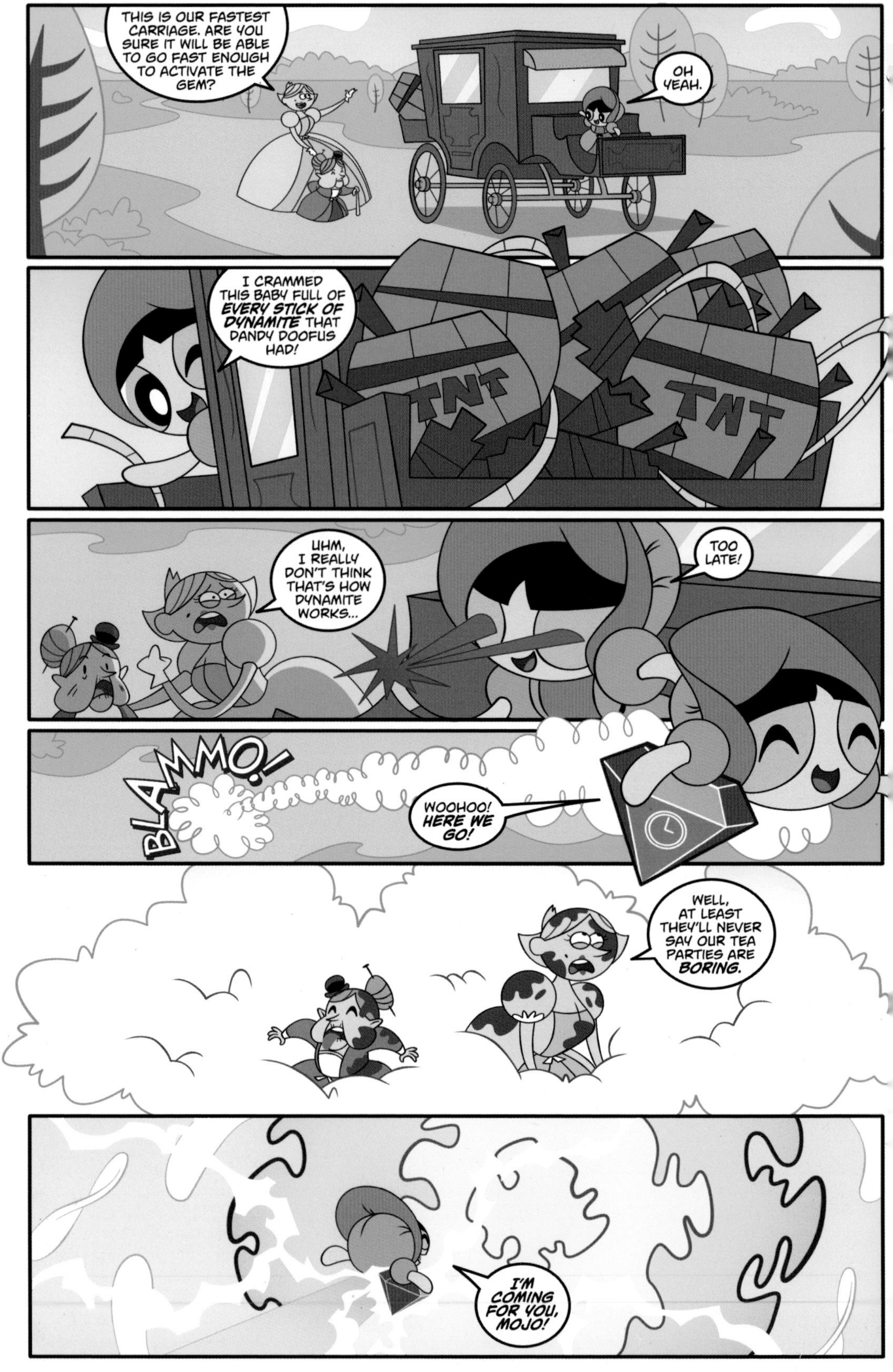
THIS IS OUR FASTEST CARRIAGE. ARE YOU SURE IT WILL BE ABLE TO GO FAST ENOUGH TO ACTIVATE THE GEM?
OH YEAH.
I CRAMMED THIS BABY FULL OF ***EVERY STICK OF DYNAMITE*** THAT DANDY DOOFUS HAD!
TNT
TNT
UHM, I REALLY DON'T THINK THAT'S HOW DYNAMITE WORKS...
TOO LATE!
BLAMMO!
WOOHOO! ***HERE WE GO!***
WELL, AT LEAST THEY'LL NEVER SAY OUR TEA PARTIES ARE ***BORING.***
I'M COMING FOR YOU, MOJO!

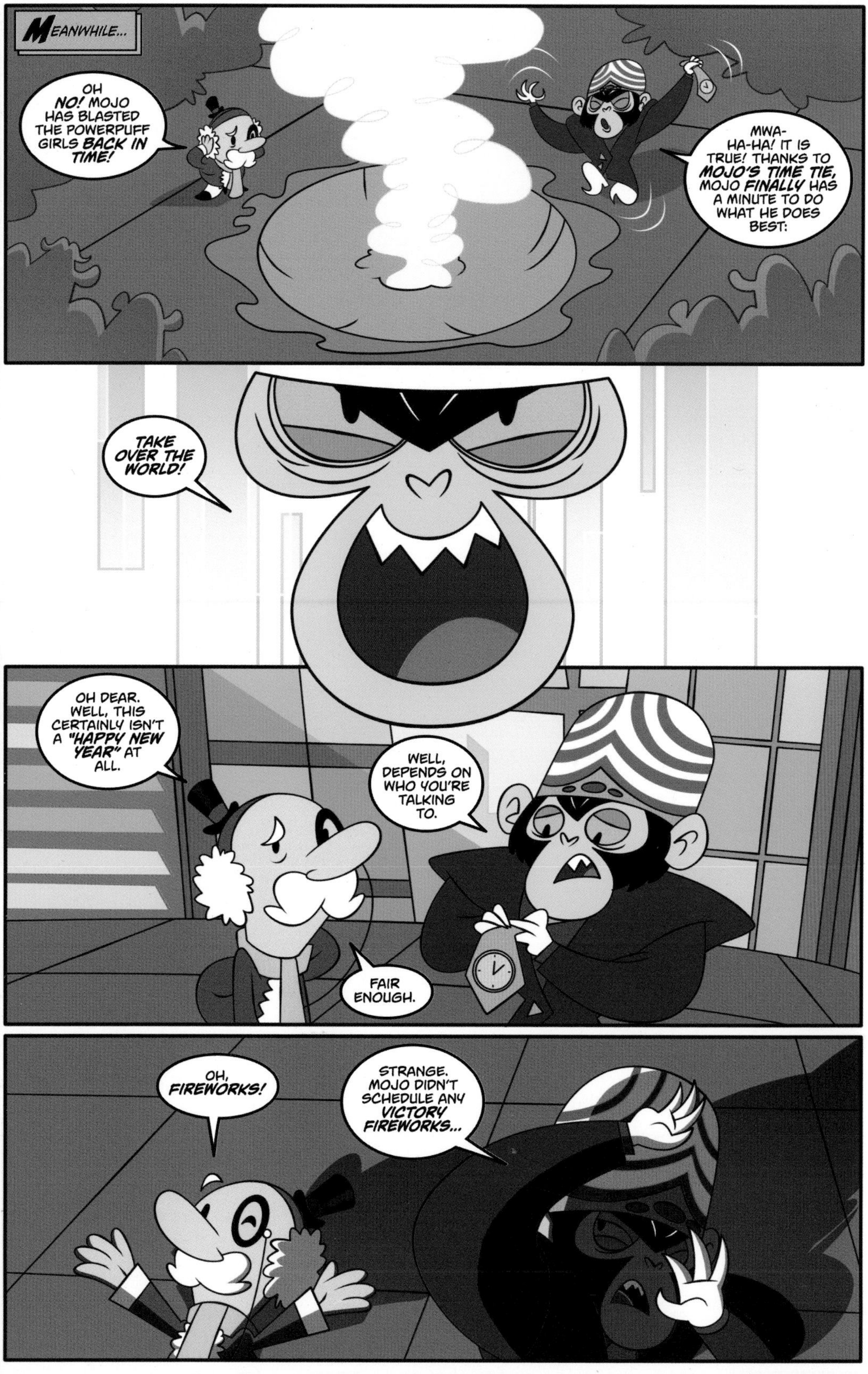
MEANWHILE...
OH NO! MOJO HAS BLASTED THE POWERPUFF GIRLS BACK IN TIME!
MWA-HA-HA! IT IS TRUE! THANKS TO MOJO'S TIME TIE, MOJO FINALLY HAS A MINUTE TO DO WHAT HE DOES BEST:
TAKE OVER THE WORLD!
OH DEAR. WELL, THIS CERTAINLY ISN'T A "HAPPY NEW YEAR" AT ALL.
WELL, DEPENDS ON WHO YOU'RE TALKING TO.
FAIR ENOUGH.
OH, FIREWORKS!
STRANGE. MOJO DIDN'T SCHEDULE ANY VICTORY FIREWORKS...

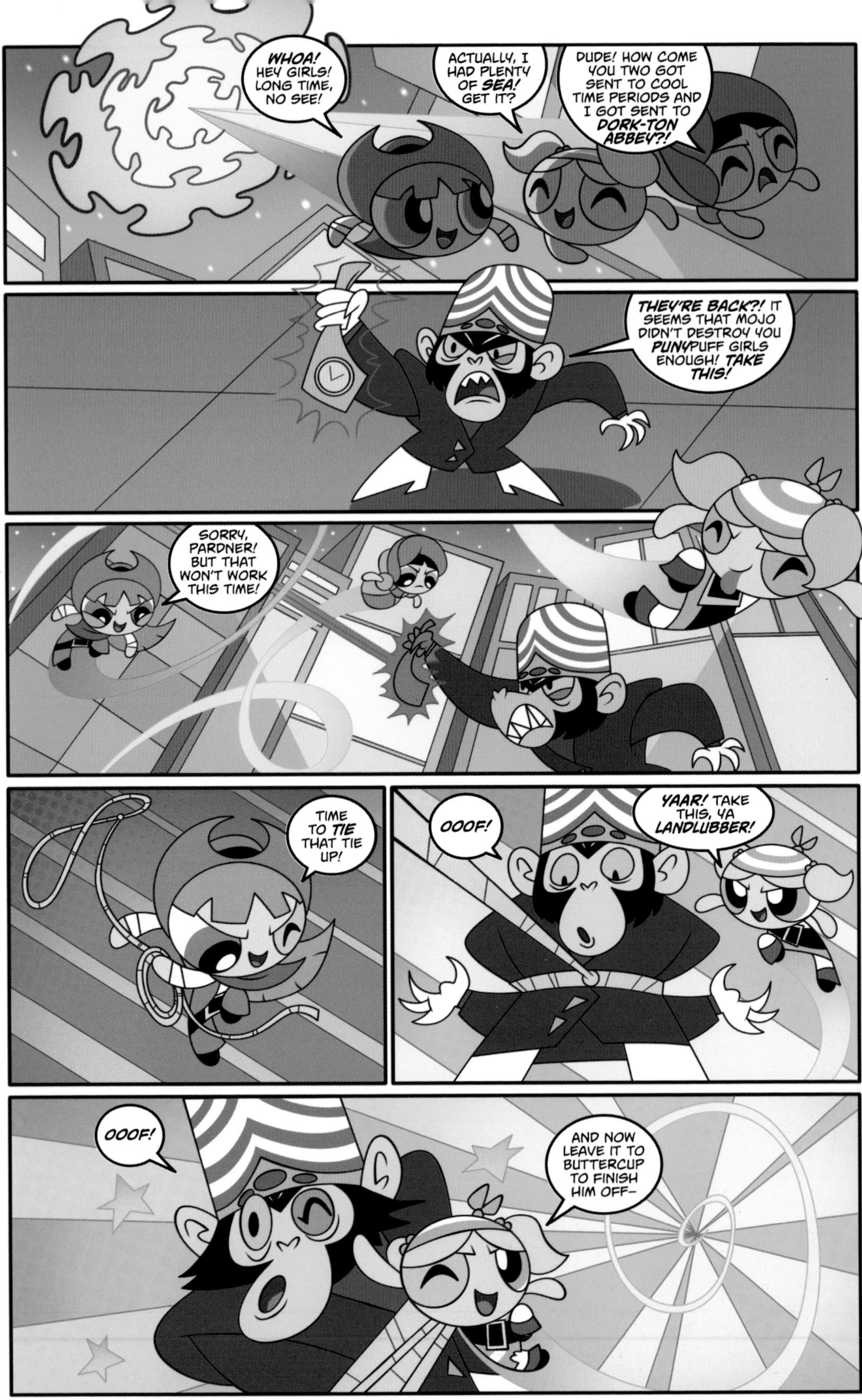
WHOA! HEY GIRLS! LONG TIME, NO SEE!
ACTUALLY, I HAD PLENTY OF SEA! GET IT?
DUDE! HOW COME YOU TWO GOT SENT TO COOL TIME PERIODS AND I GOT SENT TO DORK-TON ABBEY?!
THEY'RE BACK?! IT SEEMS THAT MOJO DIDN'T DESTROY YOU PUNY PUFF GIRLS ENOUGH! TAKE THIS!
SORRY, PARDNER! BUT THAT WON'T WORK THIS TIME!
TIME TO TIE THAT TIE UP!
OOOF!
YAAR! TAKE THIS, YA LANDLUBBER!
OOOF!
AND NOW LEAVE IT TO BUTTERCUP TO FINISH HIM OFF–

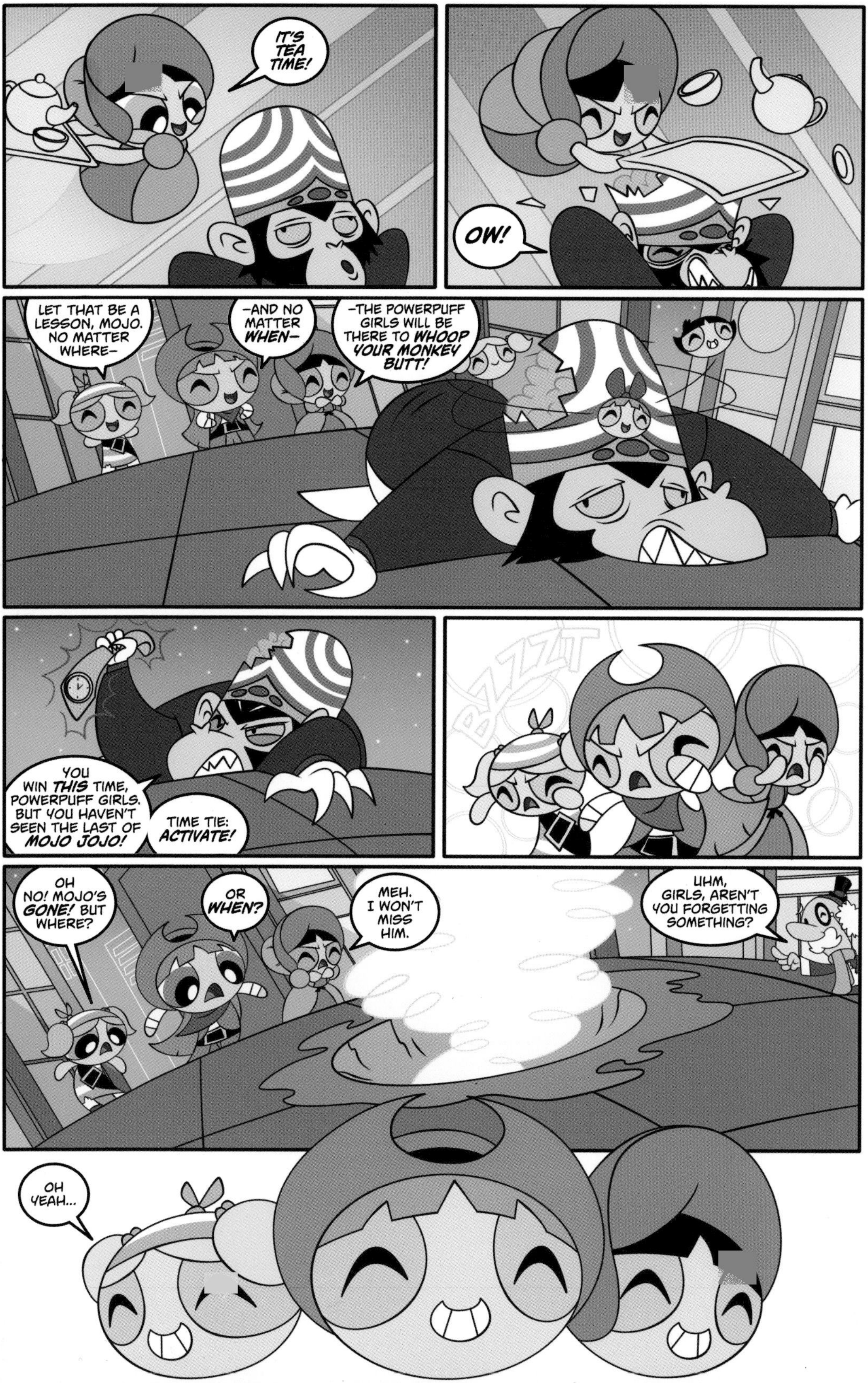

IT'S TEA TIME!
OW!
LET THAT BE A LESSON, MOJO. NO MATTER WHERE–
–AND NO MATTER WHEN–
–THE POWERPUFF GIRLS WILL BE THERE TO WHOOP YOUR MONKEY BUTT!
YOU WIN THIS TIME, POWERPUFF GIRLS. BUT YOU HAVEN'T SEEN THE LAST OF MOJO JOJO!
TIME TIE: ACTIVATE!
BZZZZT
OH NO! MOJO'S GONE! BUT WHERE?
OR WHEN?
MEH. I WON'T MISS HIM.
UHM, GIRLS, AREN'T YOU FORGETTING SOMETHING?
OH YEAH...

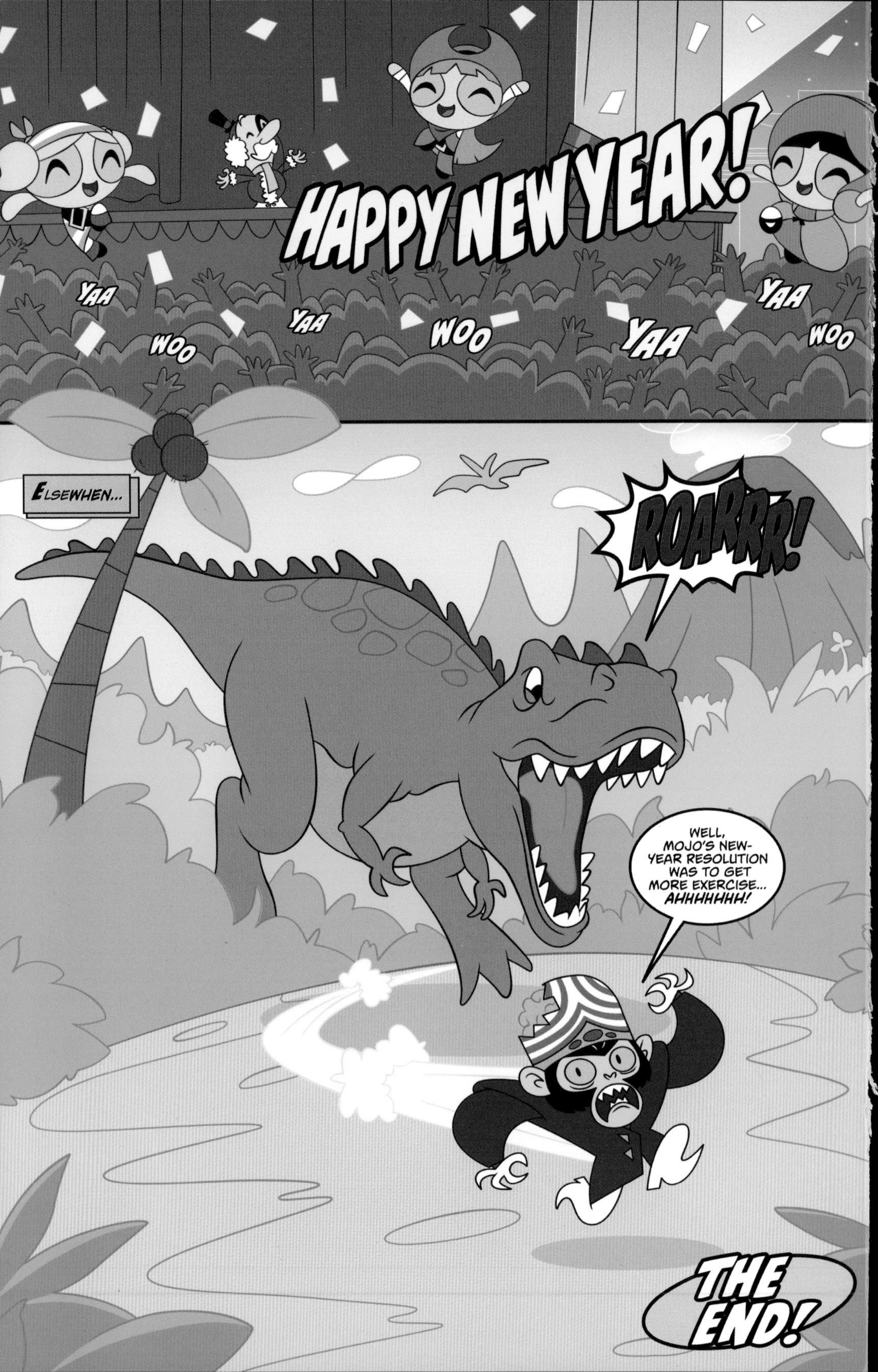
HAPPY NEW YEAR!
YAA
WOO
YAA
WOO
YAA
YAA
WOO
ELSEWHEN...
ROARRR!
WELL, MOJO'S NEW-YEAR RESOLUTION WAS TO GET MORE EXERCISE... AHHHHHHH!
THE END!

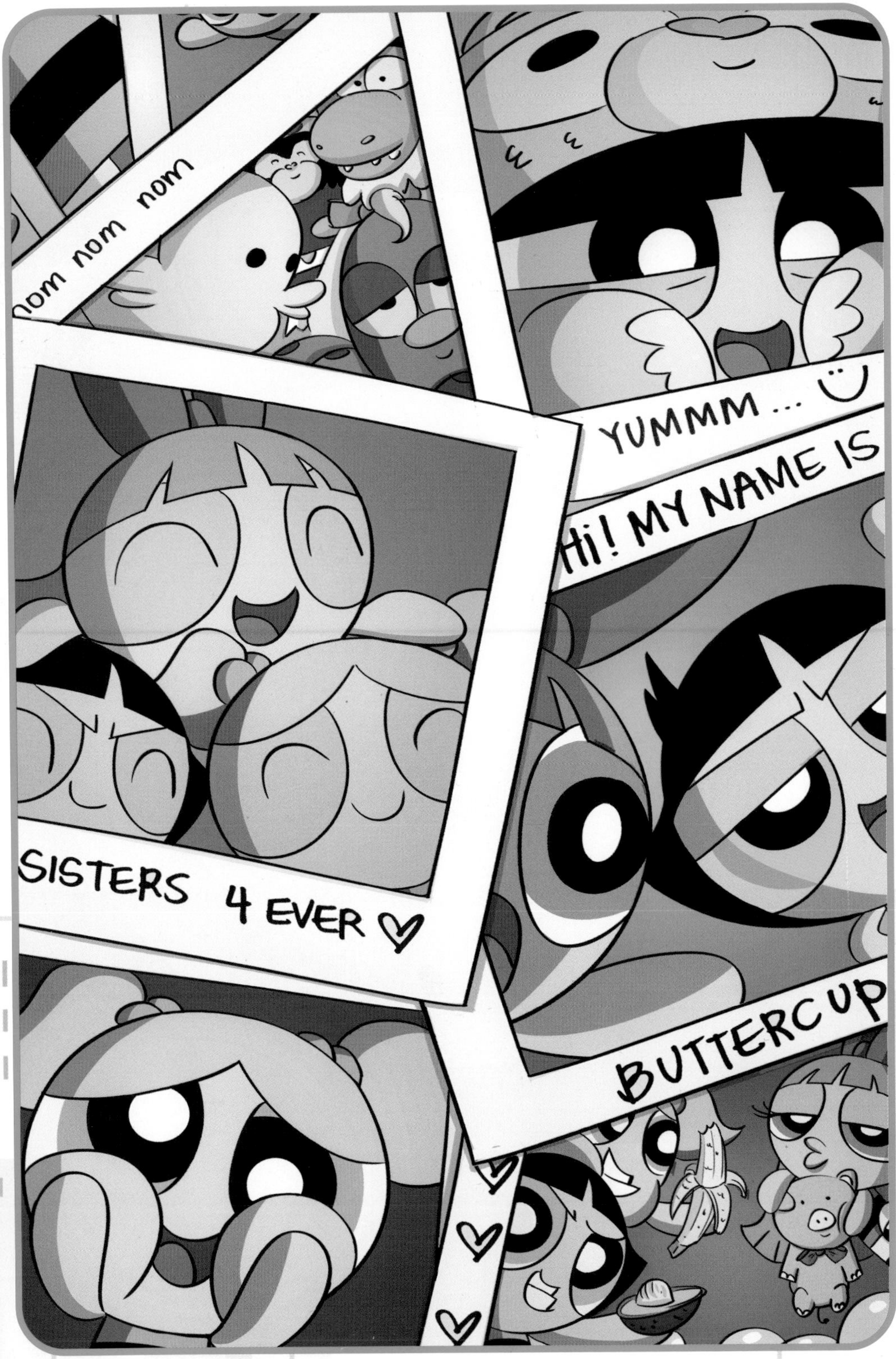
nom nom nom nom
YUMMM ...
Hi! MY NAME IS
BUTTERCUP
SISTERS 4 EVER

Cover Art by **Andy Cung**

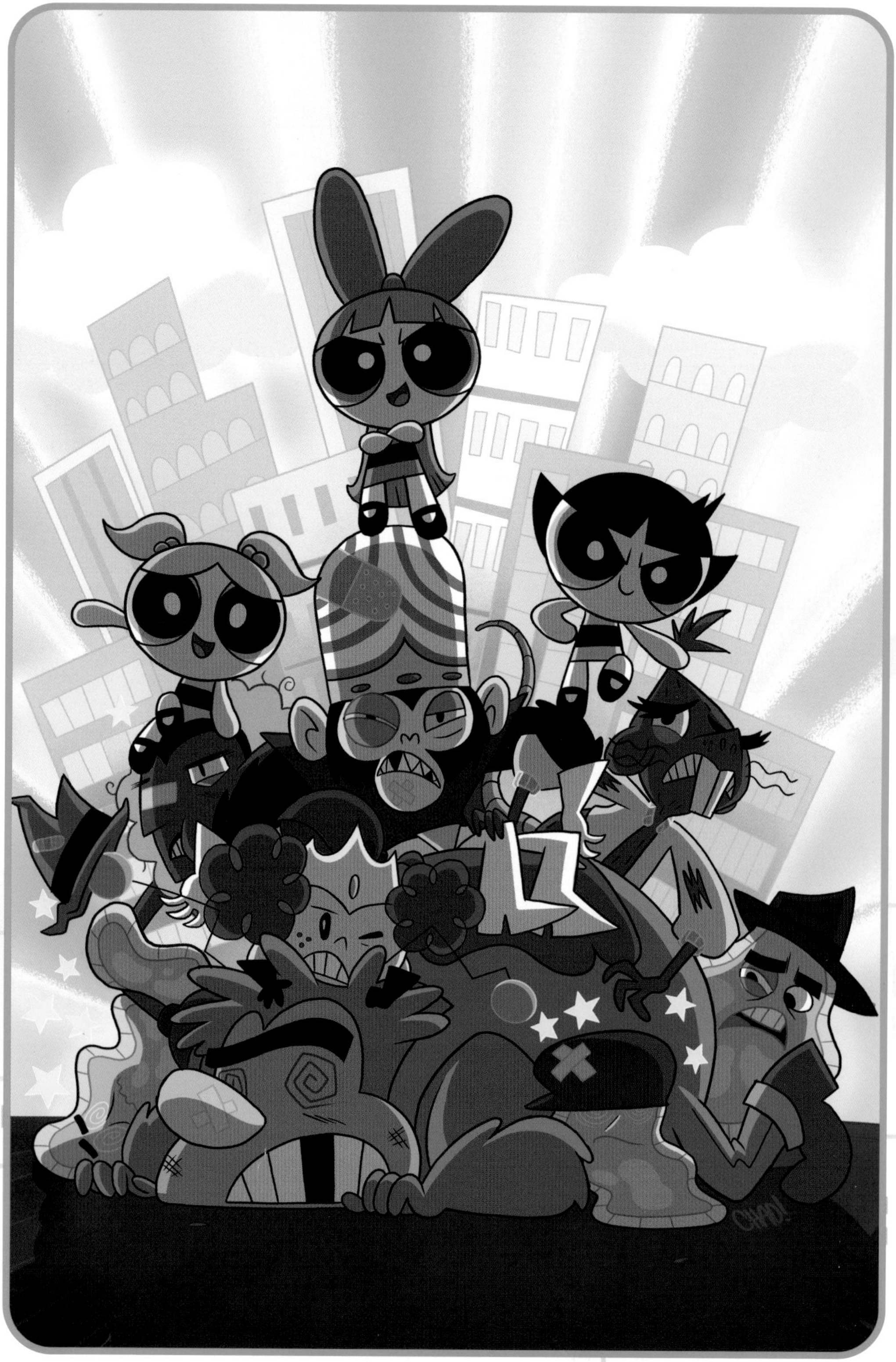

Cover Art by **Chad Thomas**

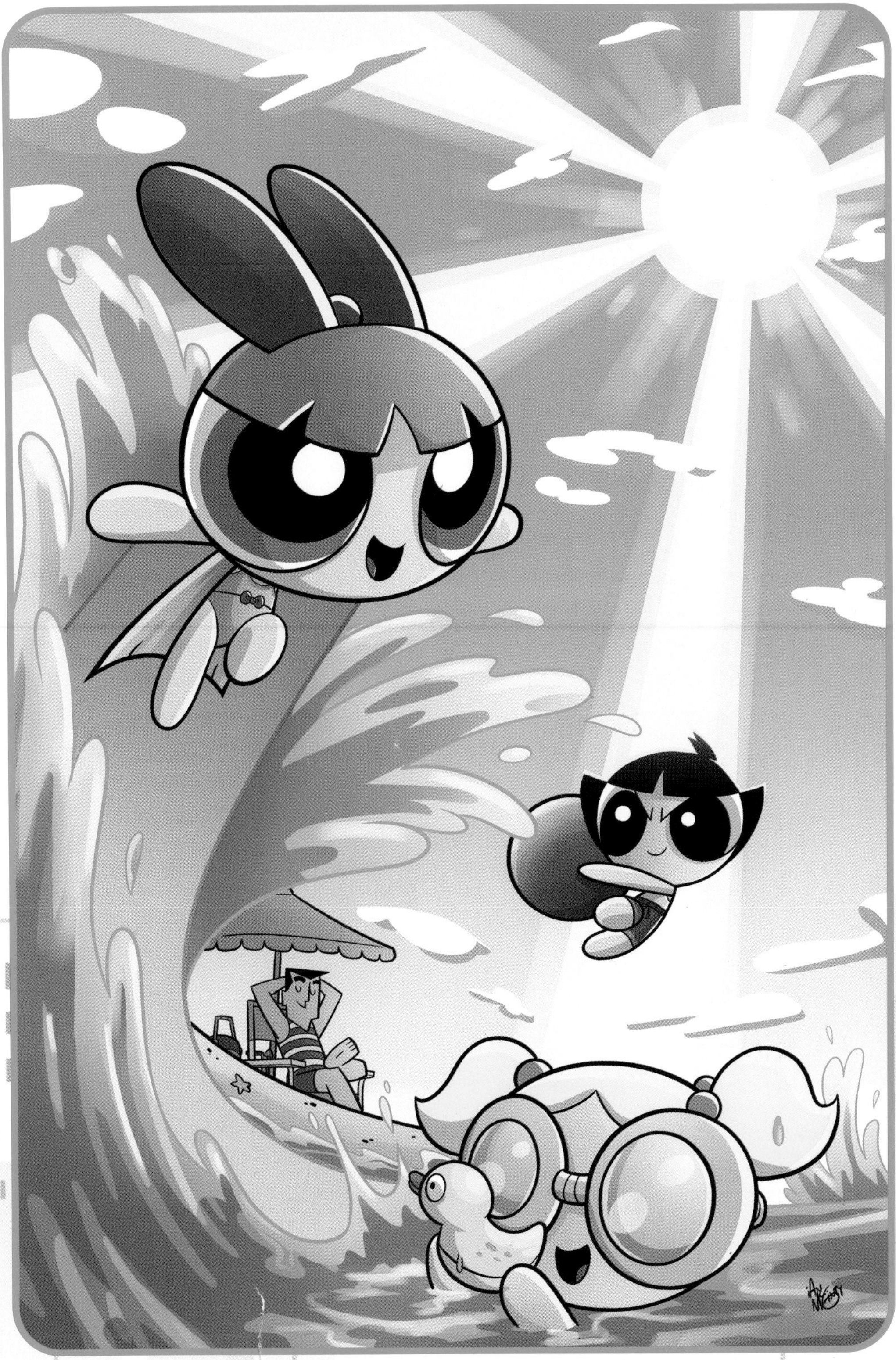

Cover Art by **Ian McGinty** Colors by **Fred** and **Meg Stresing**

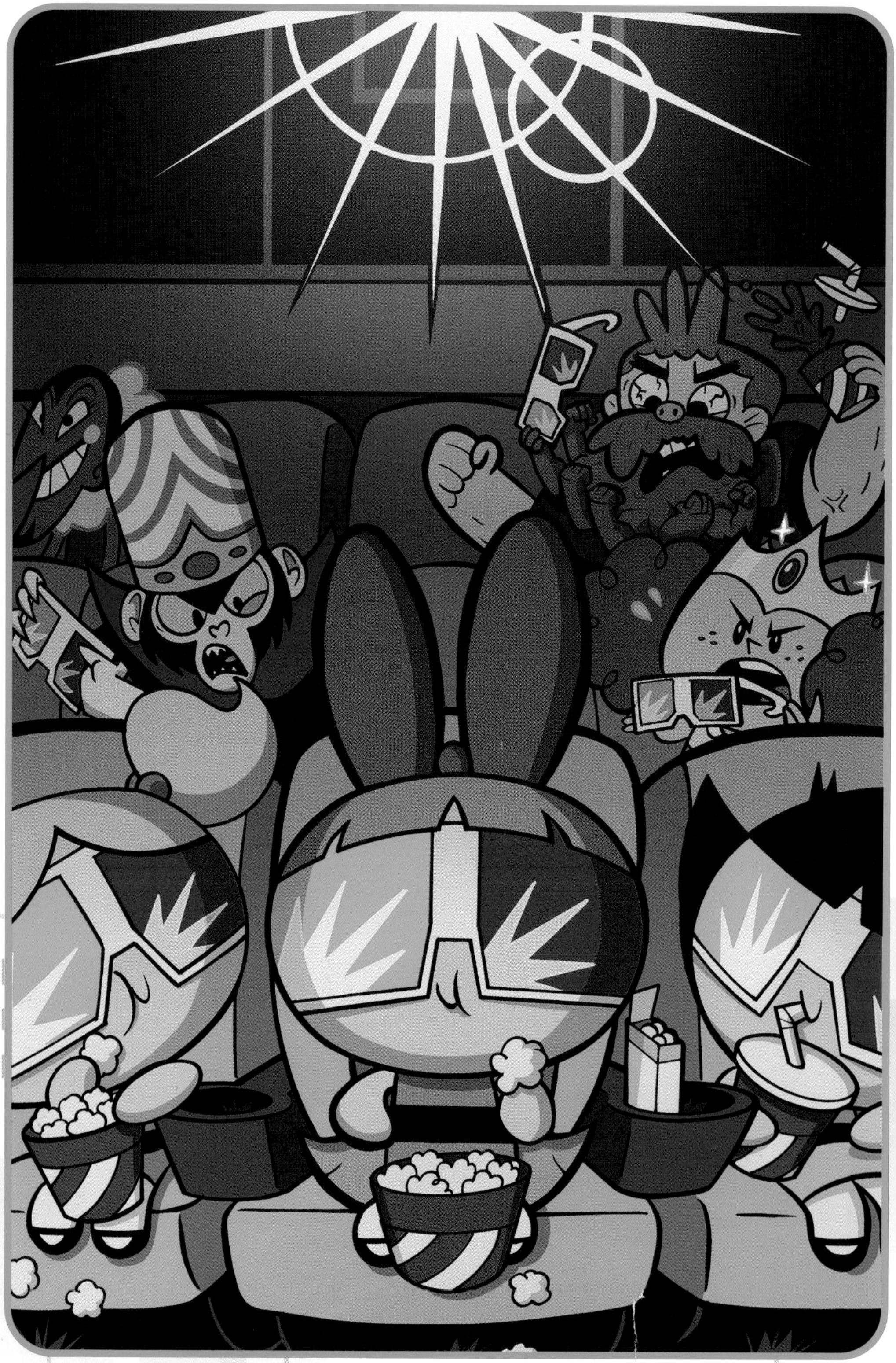

Cover Art by **Jarrett Williams**

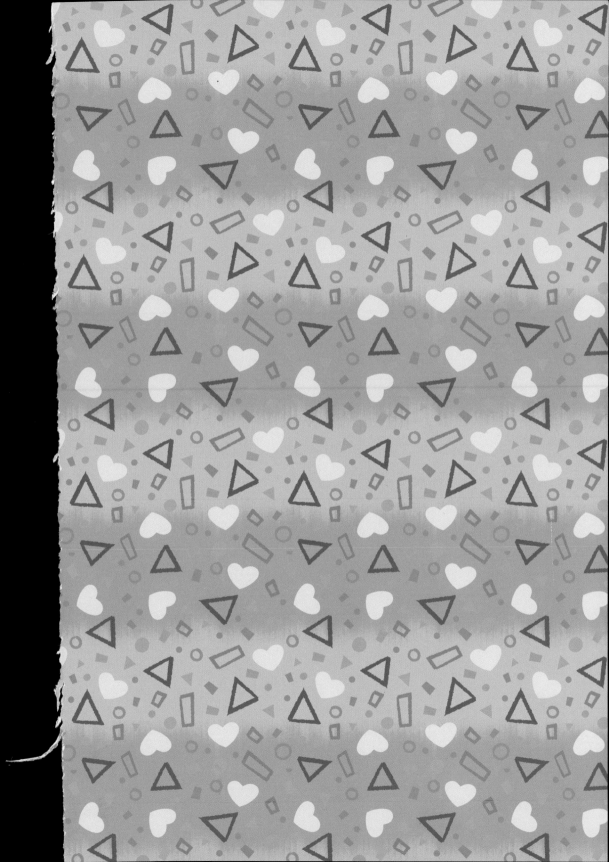

LUN
May 2018